THE SECRET
OF MAGO CASTLE

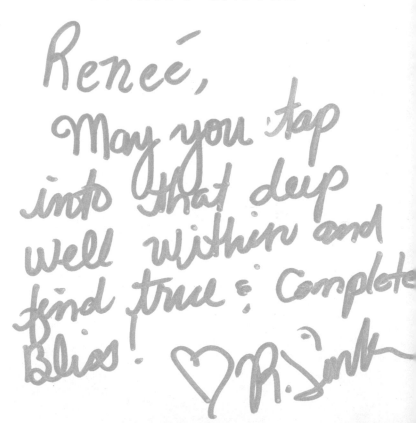

Reneé,
May you tap
into that deep
well within and
find true & Complete
Bliss!

bliss!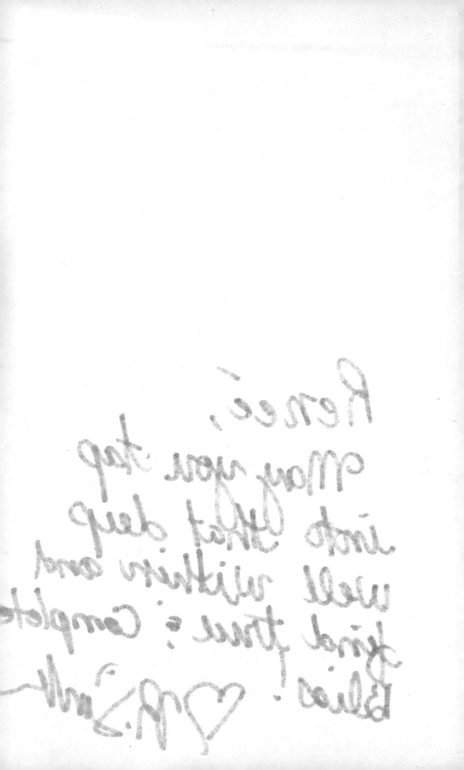

THE SECRET
OF MAGO CASTLE

REBECCA TINKLE

BEST
LIFE
MEDIA

Best Life Media
6560 AZ State Route 179
Suite 114
Sedona, AZ 86351
www.bestlifemedia.com
877.504.1106

First paperback edition: September 2014
Library of Congress Control Number: 2014946378
ISBN-13: 978-1-935127-71-0

Cover painting by Oliver Nasteski
Cover and interior design by Vanessa Maynard

For my Dumbledore

ᵥ

NOTE FROM THE AUTHOR

As an outsider looking into the Korean culture, I've been enchanted by a people who have demonstrated a truly great spirit, despite generations of adversity. I was curious to know the legends and ancient histories that shaped their spirit, so I went all the way back to the beginning, to their genesis story, for insight. What I found was a story so alive, so ripe with universal wisdom, that simply knowing it transformed me. In it, I found both a mirror for my true self and the answer to the secret longings of my heart. Through it, the way I saw myself and my world evolved.

My imagination was so taken that I discussed the details of this story with everyone I encountered. I was shocked to discover that many Koreans didn't know the full breadth of it, because much of their history and related literature had been destroyed and rewritten by the Japanese when Korea was colonized. Disheartened that this beautiful Korean story had become an echo from the past, I convinced myself that it should be known, not only by Koreans, but by all humankind, because it's just that fascinating—so I picked up my pen and went to work.

Much like my first book, *Eve*, a work of fiction exploring the creation story of my own Judeo-Christian ancestors, *The Secret of Mago Castle* is set in both modern and ancient times. It is my greatest wish that in these pages you find the same wellspring that I found the day I discovered this fresh take on what it means to be a human being. May your heart be inspired by this story of our return to the divinity within.

Rebecca Tinkle
Sedona, Arizona
June 2014

CHAPTER ONE

"Do you believe in magic?" Toby slammed another shot of whiskey down his throat and banged the glass on the table.

"Dude. Seriously," Martin yelled over the loud tribal music. "Tell me your secret."

"Magic," Toby said, spinning the shot glass between his fingers. His mood turned dark. "But even with all of the magic in the world, stuff still ain't right."

"What's not right, man?" Martin opened his arms to showcase the VIP lounge of the most popular nightclub in Manhattan. "You have everything."

Toby poured himself another shot from the bottle on the table and looked around the nightclub. A redhead at the bar beckoned him with her eyes, chewing on her straw seductively. Her weight swayed to one hip as she crossed her legs, which were wrapped like a birthday present in sheer hosiery.

"It's time for me to open my gift." Toby slapped Martin on the shoulder and rose from the booth. Straightening his tie, he went to fetch the woman. He looked exactly how a big shot analyst on Wall Street should look. His short-cropped dishwater-blonde hair was styled to perfection. His closely fitted suit high-lighted a body he spent hours a day sculpting at the gym. His blue eyes sparked with intelligence. He was concise and precise. From the outside, it appeared that he had harvested the bounty of the land, but inside, it hadn't rained in decades.

"I'm Toby," he said to the redhead with red lips.

"Jillian," she purred into his ear.

"Do you want to get out of here?"

"That depends. Where are you taking me?"

"The question isn't where I will take you, but rather what I will take you in." He held up the keys to his Ferrari.

"Your place or mine?" Her eyes flashed.

"Mine," he answered, taking her hand and pulling her to her feet.

CHAPTER TWO

"Nana!" Toby shot up in his bed, awakening from a dream.

Toby was relieved when the redhead beside him didn't stir. He couldn't remember her name. He slipped out of the bed and quietly closed the door behind him. He poured himself a drink and picked up the suit jacket he had discarded, reaching his fingers into the hidden compartment sewn into the lining and retrieving the little bronze mirror his grandmother had given him.

His mother died when he was eight years old. Unable to cope, his father had drowned himself in a bottle of whiskey. It took a while for the state to step in and transfer the guardianship of his young life to his Nana. For three long years, he teetered between complete negligence and his father's drunken rants. When he moved in with his grandmother, it took him a while to learn to trust again. His confidence in their relationship was strengthened by homework and little afterschool sandwiches with the crust trimmed off. He learned to love her, despite the fact that she embarrassed him in the supermarket and drove slower than molasses in her beat-up old station wagon, which caused him to be late to school almost every day.

He knew his heart had been completely restored by her love when he felt comfortable practicing his '*Will you go to the prom with me?*' speech on her because he was nervous about asking the most popular girl in school to be his date. He and his Nana had developed into quite the duo.

Just when he was certain that life would be good, the fates, once again, turned. Nana passed away during his senior year of high school. He came home after football practice to find her lying on the kitchen floor in a pool of urine. Once more, he was on his own.

Ever since his grandmother's death, Toby had dreamed about her. At first, he replayed sweet dreams in his mind to recapture a fleeting moment of her presence. She held his hand and counseled him as they walked slowly through the ballpark at dusk. She sat in the old rocking chair on the porch and told him how proud she was when he was accepted at Harvard. She carefully considered every pretty girl in the neighborhood and suggested that Toby take her favorite to the movies.

It was only when he started using his gift to make trades on Wall Street that she began to look at him with accusation blazing in her eyes. Toby knew it wasn't rational, but he was almost convinced that his sweet old grandma was really a witch who watched his every move and haunted his dream-time from the great beyond.

He stared down at the brass mirror, which was the size of a thimble, age-worn and round. It looked like a trinket you would find on a back shelf at an antique shop, so small and dingy that if you were to find it on the street, you would pick it up and throw it in the trash bin. But it wasn't trash; it was the single source of his power and success. Another reason why he thought his grandmother might be a witch.

"Couldn't sleep?" The redhead came out of the bedroom wearing his shirt.

"No." He took a sip of his whiskey.

She sat in his lap and took the cup from his hand, taking a long gulp.

"What's this?" She touched the tiny mirror with her fingertip.

"Don't touch that," Toby growled territorially.

"What is it?" Her interest was piqued.

"It's nothing," he answered.

When he held the mirror, he could read a person's innermost thoughts. They scrolled across their foreheads like the news ticker streaming at the bottom of a broadcast, spelling out every little secret. Most of the time, he preferred not to know what was going on in the murky minds around him, but every once in a while he read something that was paramount to him acquiring more wealth. This little mirror had been the key to his success.

"And no, it's not drugs," he answered her thoughts.

"Well then, what is it?" She leaned in seductively.

"It's none of your business." He swept her into his arms and carried her into the bedroom.

CHAPTER THREE

Leuters examined the private ten-by-ten concrete room and located a gray track suit folded on a steel table. He picked up the cotton and touched it to his nose. He hadn't smelled the subtle fragrance of dryer sheets in six months. He had spent the last months of his life smelling feet, varying degrees of body odor and grime in a Mexican federal prison. He stepped out of the worn orange jumpsuit and slipped his naked body into the soft jersey tracksuit, carefully folding the faded orange canvas and placing it on the table. As of today, he was a free man.

The door to the cell opened.

"Are you ready, Dr. Garcia?" The prison guard stepped into the room.

"Yes." He nodded and placed his hands in front of

his body to be cuffed.

Federal prison in Mexico was worse than he could have imagined, though to be honest he hadn't spent much of his life as a priest envisioning what prison would be like. His general impression about incarceration was that it was the way beasts would live, if they lived in hell, and he was ready to put it all behind him. He was genuinely relieved when his foot stepped outside the perimeter of the correctional institution.

He was greeted by his protégé and dearest friend.

"*Amigo*." Carlos embraced him, speaking in their mother tongue. "You are a free man."

"*Gracias*, Carlos." Leuters fought back tears at the sight of his friend.

"You look like a bear." Carlos tugged on Leuters's facial hair.

Leuters laughed heartily. His appearance had changed while in prison. He had grown a beard that covered his jawline in grizzly black curls, and his six-foot-five frame was, indeed, more burly. He had forgone the razor and picked up the weights.

"I will take you to your *casa* to get cleaned up." Carlos patted him on the back and led him to the car. "But brace yourself, brother. The *Subsecretaría de Regulación y Fomento Sanitario Secretaría de Salud*

(SSA) has taken everything."

Leuters nodded his head and looked out the window. "I will leave that worry for another day." He rolled down the window and felt the breeze on his face. "This moment will be spent enjoying my freedom."

***

Leuters stood in the living room of his simple *casa* in Cancun. The empty space no longer felt like his home. He imagined the raid that led to the desecration of his sanctuary: his treasured artwork commandeered from the walls, wrapped and packed into crates by men in latex gloves; the papers on his desk swept into boxes and carried away by SSA agents; beakers and chemicals packaged into containers with the word *evidence* stamped on their side in big red letters. Carlos was correct: everything had been confiscated, with the exception of the couch sitting in the center of his living room. Everything of value, either sentimental or financial, was gone.

This catastrophe, handed out by the Mexican government, was in the name of civic safety. Leuters had unjustly been branded a mad scientist and a threat to public health because of information he had discovered that threatened to liberate people from an invisible order corrupted by greed and control.

He had never been a conspiracy theorist. Being a priest, he believed in the innate goodness of people, a belief he had come to rethink. The day before he went to prison, he had stood in this very room with a corporate spy and championed a plan to eradicate illness on the planet in a foolish and hopeful display of his own humanity. The memory of that last day of his innocence played through his mind . . . .

It had begun with the doorbell ringing.

"Can I help you?" Leuters opened the door to find a gentleman in his forties standing on his porch. He wore an expensively cut suit and held a pristine black leather briefcase.

"Yes, Dr. Garcia." He handed a business card through the crack in the door. "I am Miguel from Astra Pharmaceuticals. Are you familiar with the name?"

"Indeed, I am." Leuters opened the door and examined the logo on the card. Miguel was a representative of one of the largest pharmaceutical companies in Mexico.

"I have come to inquire about your formula, MFS." Miguel smiled.

"Please, come in." Leuters tried to temper the excitement in his voice. This opportunity was exactly what he had been praying for. "Can I offer you some coffee?"

"I would love a cup of coffee." Miguel sat on the couch.

Leuters summoned his housekeeper and requested two espressos.

"We have heard claims of extraordinary results from your MFS formula and have taken an interest," Miguel continued. He retrieved a handheld recording device and, setting it on the table, asked, "Do you mind if I record our conversation?"

"Of course not," Leuters conceded, oblivious to the detrimental effects of this singular allowance.

"How did you discover it?" Miguel asked as he pressed the Record button on the device.

"I am an ordained priest," Leuters explained. "Two years ago, I accepted a mission to provide medical relief to a small village in Africa. After only three months of service, I contracted malaria. The fever consumed me, and I was in the throes of near-death delusions. Clinging desperately to life, I begged a young village boy for help. He ran for two days to seek assistance from a shaman in a nearby village.

"When he returned to my tent a few days later, I was at death's door. He was successful in retrieving the medicine but, being a young boy, he had forgotten the specific measurements to administer. There was no time to seek clarification, so he mixed the ingredients to the best of his ability, poured the liquid into my mouth, and hoped for the best. The next day, my health had been completely restored; it was as if I had never been ill. In fact, I felt better than I had in twenty years." He clapped his hands once with triumph. "That was my first experience with MFS."

"Can you walk me through the process from that initial experience to deciding to manufacture MFS?"

"It was an easy decision. Without a moment of hesitation, I gave up my position with the Church and focused exclusively on developing MFS. Spiritual health is important but physical health is the vehicle that provides the opportunity for spiritual growth. If you don't have health, you don't have anything."

"And what of your medical research?" Miguel asked, as he wrote a few notes on a pad of paper.

"I experimented with the applications of the solution myself. It had a positive effect on everything from rashes to tooth infections, allergies and common colds."

"Have any other experiences been quantified?" Miguel set his pen on the tablet and picked up his coffee.

"A few of the tribe members with terminal diseases volunteered to try the formula. We found that in many cases both cancer and HIV could be eradicated from the body with the use of this solution, as well. That is why I have dedicated my efforts to further exploring its capabilities. With the proper funding, we have the potential to completely transform the current plight of insufficient healthcare on the planet. And the best part is that the ingredients are so common that it can be produced and distributed for pennies to everyone on the planet."

"That is quite a claim." Miguel smiled.

"I assure you, it is more than just a claim. Would you like to try a little for yourself?" Leuters offered.

"Oh, no thank you," Miguel declined politely. "I'm here strictly on a fact-finding mission."

"Is Astra Pharmaceuticals interested in purchasing this formula for development?" Leuters leaned forward in anticipation.

"Among other things. But before I get ahead of myself, I must admit that we are merely in the investigation stage." Miguel cleared his throat and stood. "I think that I have enough here. We will be in contact to let you know the next step." He smiled disingenuously and shook Leuters's hand.

The next day, a warrant had been issued for Leuters' immediate arrest. He went to trial in front of a judge the same day and was sentenced to six months in prison. There was no jury of his peers. In the following months, his medical license was stripped, and he was demonized in the press with misconstrued half-truths about his endeavors.

Leuters had replayed that fateful meeting in his mind a thousand times while imprisoned. The subtle clues of his imminent damnation were present in the meeting, but his impassioned enthusiasm for worldwide progression compelled him to ignore that whisper of intuition. He had vowed never to make that mistake again as long as he lived.

"We'll have to start all over again," Carlos said, sitting beside him on the couch.

"There is nothing to start," Leuters despaired, looking around the empty room.

"But we have to finish your work," Carlos protested.

"Illegally producing MFS carries a penalty more severe than distributing street narcotics. It is finished," Leuters told his old friend with finality.

"There are many people counting on you, brother." Carlos touched his shoulder.

"It causes me great remorse to tell you that we must cease our work," Leuters said quietly. "You have no idea what it was like in there."

"But the world needs MFS," Carlos protested.

"The government has made it clear that our efforts would be dealt with harshly." He sighed. "We have made very powerful enemies."

A spirited knock at the door was followed by multiple rings of the doorbell in a jolly rhythm. Leuters opened the door and was met with a crowd holding balloons and cakes, escorted by a *mariachi* band playing a hearty tune. Two young boys held a sign that read, *Welcome Home, Hero.*

Tears touched Leuters's eyes. Carlos put his hand on his shoulder again.

"The people of our village have pooled their money so that you may begin again."

Leuters looked at the hopeful faces of his greatest supporters in the community and his heart, which had closed during his incarceration, opened again. He remembered the reason that he had been eager to share MFS far and wide in the first place. It was the people. He stepped aside and waved the party into his house.

"Come in, come in!" he laughed.

"Have you changed your mind?" Carlos asked after the sea of people had passed.

"If we do this, it is at great risk. If the SSA finds out ..."

"It is a risk worth taking," Carlos assured him.

"We must go back to my village in Teotihuacán and

consult with my father. The continuance of this mission isn't one to accept lightly, my friend. Six months in prison was a warning to a foolish idealist. If we proceed, we will be sending a message of defiance that will provoke the wrath of a very powerful group of people," Leuters promised, closing the door behind them.

CHAPTER FOUR

Leuters and Carlos walked the property of his child-hood home under the bright midday sun. The spray of mist from the fountains chilled their flesh, while the heat from the ground scorched through the soles of their sandals as if they walked upon the sun itself. The estate expanded as far as the eye could see. The only distinct identifier of the property's boundary was the pyramids of Teotihuacán that rose majestically on the horizon. The main housing structure looked more like a palace than a home.

Carlos looked around the property with acute fascination. "This is where you grew up?" he asked in disbelief.

"After my parents died, I was adopted by a great man and this became my home." Leuters looked around the estate where he had played hide-and-seek as a young boy amid the many fountains and statues.

"This was my family." They stopped in front of a pristine white stone effigy. Two parents and two children stood as a family unit. The mother's palms rested serenely on her children's shoulders while the father's arm wrapped around her waist protectively. The children's faces shone with health and happiness.

"How did they die?" Carlos asked quietly.

"I lost them to drugs." Leuters touched the face of his mother's image lightly.

"This doesn't look like a family who lived in the slums," Carlos pondered.

"Quauhtli—my adopted father—made this statue to honor the life they deserved." Leuters turned to Carlos. "He was compassionate to the plight of my family and wanted to ensure that I would remember the divinity of my family of origin, instead of the hardships of the street life that I had endured."

"You were very lucky to have found him."

"It was he who found me," Leuters whispered. "That day my life began."

"How did you meet?" Carlos asked as they resumed their stride to the main house.

Leuters pointed to the stone structures on the horizon. "I was playing on the temples of Teotihuacán."

As Leuters recounted that fateful day, the memory unfolded in his mind. He was fully there, a six-year-old boy who ran noisily through the stone pyramids, using a branch as a makeshift sword to defeat an invisible dragon.

"I will defeat you!" He stabbed the air in front of him. "You evil dragon. You have met with the greatest swordsman in all of Teotihuacán!"

"Confounding child!" the voice of an old man exclaimed from the pyramid stairs.

"State your business!" Leuters exclaimed, holding the point of his branch in Quauhtli's direction. "Friend or foe?"

The old man laughed. "You make so much noise that you will wake the gods!" He hobbled down the stairs. When he came upon Leuters, a look of delight passed his features. "Ah, I think I see one now." He looked directly into Leuters's eyes.

"Where?" Leuters looked behind him.

"Inside of you, young boy. You don't know it now, but God sleeps inside of you." The old man leaned down to whisper in his ear, "You will save the world."

Leuters saluted as if he were a disciplined guard, holding his small frame upright.

"You are very dirty; where are your parents?"

"Over there," Leuters lied.

"Let me meet them."

They walked around the pyramids, searching for a family that didn't exist because Leuters was too ashamed to admit he was alone in the world.

"Have you lied to me?" the old man asked.

Leuters shifted his small head down in shame.

"Where are your parents?" He knelt to look in Leuters's eyes.

"They are dead," Leuters confessed quietly.

The man passed his hand over the top of Leuters's head. "I will awaken the divinity within you, so that you will remember you are a child of God and not a child of circumstance. Until you are old enough to pro-vide for yourself, I will provide for you."

The memory faded and Leuters was brought back to the moment. That was a long time ago, yet he could remember it as clearly as yesterday. Some memories didn't fade with time.

"What happened to your brother?" Carlos asked, looking at the statue.

"Alexandro? I don't know," Leuters whispered. "Quauhtli and I returned to the slums to find him, but he'd disappeared." His voice quivered. "The loss of my brother has been the single greatest wound in my heart. I can only imagine the type of life he lived out there on his own."

"You feel guilty for being raised in such lavishness by a loving father?" Carlos asked.

"It's the reason that I became a doctor and a priest. To help the people who weren't as lucky as me. I have never forgotten my roots. I have never forgotten my brother."

"Can this be?" The delighted voice of an old man echoed through the courtyard. "Has my son returned?" His steps were small as he shuffled toward them on quivering legs. He looked ancient.

Leuters ran to embrace him. The old man was half his height and a quarter his width.

"Okay, okay." The old man waved him off. "Don't crush me."

"Sorry, Father," Leuters laughed.

"Who is this that we have here?" Quauhtli raised his glasses to his eyes.

"Father, this is Carlos," Leuters introduced the two men. "He's an old friend of mine from Cancun."

A strange looked passed over Quauhtli's wrinkled face. "And how did you two meet?" he asked, narrowing his eyes.

"We met at a soup kitchen," Carlos explained. "Your

son took me under his wing and helped me get my life together."

"Hmmph," Quauhtli huffed. "Well, come inside. You'll bake like potatoes out here."

"Thank you, Father." Leuters took his elbow and helped the feeble old man inside.

"Now, you'll have to tell me all about jail," Quauhtli said. "I have heard quite a lot about you from the house-keepers in the past months."

"I know, Father." Leuters voice dropped. "I am sorry to have shamed you."

"No shame, no shame." He patted the back of Leuters's hand, which was secured across his old fore-arm. "What wags on the tongues of gossips rarely has anything to do with truth."

Quauhtli scrutinized Carlos with suspicious, side-ways glances. Leuters wondered if the years had af-fected his father's mind. He'd never witnessed him behave in this unwelcoming manner to any guest, whether he be a king or a criminal. He'd taught him that all men contained a spark of divinity within them and therefore all men were equal. His change in be-havior was disconcerting. When they had a moment alone, Leuters would implore that his father be kind to their houseguest.

CHAPTER FIVE

Noah challenged death every day. He was a heart surgeon, and an excellent one at that. Instinct, he called it.
But it was something more, a type of super-awareness
that warned him if he was about to make a cut even
a millimeter off its mark. This sixth sense had saved
countless lives and garnered him the reputation for being a medical master and a hero in the hearts of patients worldwide.

He unbuttoned the single button on his white lab
coat and sat in his chair with a huff. His sleep was fail-
ing to leave him refreshed. He was tired all of the time.
He rubbed his eyes.

He scanned his office, noting the many pictures with
various celebrities and politicians whose family members had been under his care. He remembered all too

clearly the boy under the suit, the awkward teenager with knobby knees, an afro, a squeaky voice and no date for prom. But that was a long time ago. He heard a soft knock on the door.

"Come in," he called, returning a photo frame to his desk.

"Dr. Whitley?" His colleague peeked his head in the door. "Am I interrupting?"

"Please come in," Noah reaffirmed sitting up in his chair. "Can I help you?"

Dr. Carey stepped into Noah's office and closed the door behind him. Noah noticed that he held a medical file close to his side almost as if to conceal it. Dr. Carey was an up-and-coming cardiothoracic surgical resident that Noah hand-picked from the intern pool many years ago. He was an intelligent young man with good hands and a cool head under pressure. He sat in the chair opposite Noah.

"Dr. Whitley." He cleared his throat nervously. "There is no easy way to say this. It might be a good idea for you to review this yourself." His hand trembled as he passed the file over the desk.

Noah's heart skipped a beat as he took the file with a firm hand. He had asked Dr. Carey to run a full battery of tests to determine the cause of his recent fatigue.

He opened the folder and reviewed the three pages of data. On the last page, he discovered the cause of his exhaustion. He sat back in his chair and tossed the file on the desk.

"I guess that solves it. Diagnosis?" he asked, with the neutral supervisorial tone that he had used on countless occasions while testing the boundaries of his intern's knowledge.

"Dr. Whitley . . ." Carey protested.

"Diagnosis," Noah insisted.

Carey answered as directed, "Patient Noah Whitley, age sixty-three, symptoms, fatigue and dizziness. Cardiac MRI and blood tests confirm severe cardiomyopathy."

"Prognosis?" Noah leaned back in his chair and tapped his pen on the desk.

"Dr. Whitley," Carey objected.

"Prognosis?" Noah asked again.

"Fatal," Carey answered quietly, shifting his eyes to the desk.

"Treatment options?"

"Transplant."

"Interim treatment?"

"Doctor recommends that patient be admitted to the hospital immediately and placed on a left ventricular assist device until a donor heart is available."

"Very good, Dr. Carey. That will be all," Noah finished, lost in thought.

CHAPTER SIX

Noah looked out the den window of the estate he and his wife had purchased when he was a young surgeon. He walked to the hearth of the fireplace and traced his fingers across the glass of the family portrait. His wife had died in a traffic accident three years earlier, leaving Noah and his daughter to fend for themselves. He retrieved his phone from his pocket and dialed.

An answering machine picked up the call.

"You have reached Annie," the lively voice of his daughter echoed in his ear.

"And Bill," her fiancé chimed in. Their two voices overlapped cutely to finish the message, "Leave a message after the tone."

"Hi, darling," Noah said, attempting to disguise the melancholy in his voice. "Just calling to check on the wedding plans."

The line clicked.

"Daddy!" she pealed with delight. "Sorry, I couldn't get to the phone in time."

"Hi, sweetheart," he said, his voice overflowing with affection.

"Darling? Sweetheart? Two terms of endearment in one call?" she chastised. "What's wrong?"

Noah laughed. "Nothing, four-eyes," he teased.

"That's more like it," she laughed airily. "What's up, Papa Bear?"

"I was just thinking of you," he answered. "And of your mother."

She was quiet for a minute.

"Are you okay, Dad?" Her voice dropped with concern.

"I was just thinking how much your mother would have loved to see you walk down the aisle in her wedding dress." His wife had been a hopeless romantic with a flair for fairy tale dramatics. She saved her dress so that she would be able to witness her daughter marry within its layers of lace and puffed sleeves. Noah never imagined that she wouldn't. As fate would have it, he might not either. Noah would trade everything that he owned to be able to have his daughter step on his toes during the traditional father-daughter reception dance.

"Have you picked a date?" he asked as casually as possible.

"Right away," she answered. "I'm pretty sure that I can pull together a modern-day wedding miracle in three months if I focus on nothing else."

Noah wondered if he had three months.

"Why not sooner?" he suggested. "Maybe on a beach in Hawaii?"

"Daddy!" she squealed. "Three months *is* fast. What's the hurry—you're not tired of me already, are you?"

"I will never tire of you, Annie," he promised.

Orphan Annie. The thought of it made him sick.

"I need at least three months. I have to find the venue, hire a caterer, have my dress altered, send invitations . . . and Bill can't take time away for the honeymoon in the middle of the school year." She was appalled that her father, who hadn't missed a day of work in years, would possibly suggest that her fiancé miss a single day of work at the local middle school where he taught the sixth grade, much less two entire weeks.

"It was just a thought," he said in a reassuring voice.

His heart squeezed in his chest. Twisted, actually.

He struggled to catch his breath.

He knew the signs. His left arm tingled.

"Annie," he said smoothly. "I have to get off

the phone now."

"That's okay. Bill just walked through the door."

"Goodbye, sweetheart. I love you." He fought to keep his voice composed through the pain.

"Bye, Daddy."

Noah hung up the phone, dialed 911, and reached into his desk drawer to retrieve a bottle of aspirin. He popped five tablets into his mouth and chewed as he slumped into the old leather desk chair, praying the ambulance reached him in time.

CHAPTER SEVEN

Angeline woke with a start. She looked at the clock—four in the morning and threw herself back into her pillow, knowing she would lie awake until her alarm buzzed in three hours. She always had trouble falling back asleep after a nightmare. But it wasn't really a nightmare that she had woken from; it was a memory that had replayed itself in a continuous loop over the past twenty years of sleep.

It was always the same.

"Where do babies come from?" Angeline asked with her puny four-year-old voice. She held her teddy bear tightly and twirled a single golden curl around her index finger.

Her father patted the tail end of the mare about to give birth and tipped his white cowboy hat up to meet his daughter's eyes. "From their mommy's belly." He turned his attention back to the mare whose allantois fluid poured into the surrounding hay.

"Is that where I came from?" Angeline wrinkled her nose.

"Yes, darlin'," he replied mechanically, his full attention on comforting their horse through the process of labor.

"Where did you come from, Daddy?"

"I came from my mommy's belly," he answered patiently.

"Grandma?"

"That's right." He sighed.

"Where did Grandma come from?"

"Angeline," her father rebuked her sternly, "Shouldn't you be in bed?"

"But I want to stay with Princess. She needs me."

Princess kicked all four legs and wailed.

"What's wrong with Princess, Daddy?" She furrowed her brow.

"Wait outside the stable!" he barked impatiently.

Although she was scared by her father's severe command, her feet quickly carried her outside of the stall—but no further. She couldn't leave without making sure that Princess was okay. She pressed her eye to a small crack in the door and watched as her father stuck his arm up the back end of her favorite pet.

"That's right, Princess, don't push just yet," he said in a calm reassuring voice. "I just need to reposition your foal; she's an elbow lock. Just give it a second while I . . ." He maneuvered his arm and pushed the foal back into its womb. "That's it . . ." he cooed. "I got the second foot." He pulled the two feet, grunting from the effort.

Princess huffed as she pushed and her father puffed as he pulled.

After a few moments of cooperative effort, a white embryotic bag slipped from Princess's womb onto the hay. Her father tore open the white sack and a baby horse was revealed. The little horse was beautiful, white with tan spots. Angeline was going to name her Joy.

He wiped the foal's head with a towel and tried to rouse it, but it wouldn't stir. It lay on the ground motionless while Princess whinnied and panted unnaturally. Sensing the mare's alarm, Angeline's father rushed back to attend to Princess. He moved quickly to and fro, checking her from all sides. She moaned in a way that made Angeline's heart drop into her stomach. Her father wiped his hands on the towel and kissed her nose.

"Sorry, girl," he whispered. "I promise that I won't

let you suffer much longer."

When he stepped out of the stall, he found Angeline clutching her teddy bear with trembling arms. He knelt to his knee and pulled her close.

"I think it's time to say goodbye to Princess."

"Goodbye?" Angeline's voice quivered. "Where is she going?"

"To sleep, sweetheart."

"Then I'll just say goodnight," Angeline insisted.

Her father picked her up and sat her gently beside the horse.

"Say goodbye, sweetheart. She's going to heaven," he said quietly, standing to leave.

"Please don't go to heaven, stay here with me . . . I need you," Angeline cried. She knew from previous experiences that heaven was a place you went and never came back from. She combed Princess's mane. "Please God," she prayed. "Please God, help me."

Angeline jumped when the single lightbulb in the stall buzzed and shattered. The stall should have gone dark, but Angeline could still see because a golden hue like candlelight encapsulated both her and her horse. Princess whinnied and raised herself to her feet. She stood majestically, tall and proud, and Angeline crumpled into a ball on the floor.

"Angeline!" her father yelled, bursting into the dark stall. He held a gun over his shoulder. He shone the beam from his flashlight and found her lying nearly unconscious next to the lifeless body of the foal. Princess nuzzled her small neck. Angeline used all of her will to open her eyes and tell her father the good news.

"She's all better, Daddy," she breathed just before she lost consciousness.

CHAPTER EIGHT

"I know it isn't rational, Angeline," Michela cried. "But I'm mad at my body."

Angeline cozied herself closer to Michela on the old beige couch in her living room. She rested her head against her friend and brushed a golden curl away from her eye.

"It's understandable," Angeline offered quietly.

"I just don't know how this happened," Michela cried. "I haven't eaten sugar in over ten years, I exercise . . . I am a vegetarian, for god's sake," she huffed. "And that bastard. That selfish, brainless, heartless bastard. I'm furious with him too."

Angeline did the only thing that she knew to comfort her friend—she held her hand.

"How could he leave me . . . now?" Michela asked

despondently, turning to Angeline.

"I don't know." Angeline stroked her hair. "Maybe it's for the best. You need to focus on yourself while you go through treatment."

"I'm not going to undergo treatment, Angeline."

"What?" Angeline shot upright.

"I can't afford it," Michela confessed.

"Michela," Angeline warned. "You have to get treatment."

"It's stage four." Michela's voice dropped to a whisper. "And I'm not going to bankrupt my family with medical debt."

"But there's a chance that you'll beat it."

"A slim chance."

"You have to try."

"Why?"

"Because life is a gift."

"A rotten gift."

"Don't say that!"

"What's so great about life? Are you happy? I certainly wasn't."

"Sure, it can be hard. But you have to try."

"Give me one reason why?" Michela challenged, with the fury of a woman scorned by life.

"Because it can be better. We can make it better,"

Angeline promised, taking Michela into her arms.

Angeline's body burned hot. She felt the same golden heat emanate from her cells that she had experienced countless times before. She felt the particles conglomerate into a field of energy that enveloped Michela and knew without a doubt that she would be okay. Angeline never knew when and where this phenomenon would occur. It wasn't something she could control, even if she tried. This movement of energy wasn't the result of something that she did, it was something that moved mysteriously through her. The only thing that she knew was that she would have to pay the price. And she knew it would be a steep one.

Stage four uterine cancer.

She wondered how that was going to feel.

She wouldn't have to wait long to find out.

***

Angeline woke to the sound of the phone ringing. She looked at the calendar on her mobile phone and discovered that she had been asleep on her couch for two full days. She moaned and turned over, tying to ignore the pain that ripped through her body. Her blood hurt, like poison flowing through her veins. She held her abdomen tightly and pressed her fingers deep into her flesh, attempting to dull the sensation of a thousand undulant needles tearing her uterus from the inside out. She knew that if she could just fall asleep for a little longer she could shut down her senses and numb her mind to the agony. This was the price for her gift.

She rolled over and tried not to think. Nothing about her made sense. She was a walking, talking bundle of contradictions. She tried to present herself as a stable member of society, but she couldn't hold down a regular job because she possessed a spiritual power to draw in toxic energy and alchemize it with her body, which she knew was miraculous, but not something she could explain to employers. She couldn't parlay these abilities into a career, because they weren't consistent enough to be relied upon. She felt like a fish out of water most of the time.

Using all of the might that she could muster, she raised her phone to her ear and checked her voicemail.

"Angeline!" Michela's cheerful voice echoed in her ear. "You are never going to guess what happened. I went back to the hospital, just as you suggested, and they ran more tests . . . and the tumor is gone! They don't know what happened . . . they think maybe my test results got mixed up with another patient's. Angeline, I'm not going to die." Her bright voice pealed with delight. "Anyway, I'm going to celebrate with Claude. He's taking me to Chicago for the weekend to meet his parents! Can you believe it?"

She could believe it. In fact, she was unable to forget it as she writhed on her couch drenched in sweat.

"Call me. I don't think that I'm going to make it to our road trip." Michela's voice dropped apologetically. "Please don't be mad."

Angeline hung up the phone and it dropped to the floor with a thump.

"Please give me the strength to accept the things that I cannot change . . ." she prayed.

CHAPTER NINE

The beep of the heart monitor was music to Noah's ears. That steady rhythm was the tempo his fingers swayed to as they wove through the human heart like the skillful bow of a world-class cellist. And as with any skilled performer, the dull screech of the flatline was not an end, but rather an exciting opportunity to ensure that the symphony would carry on for the person lying on his table. His utmost passion and the reason that he became a heart surgeon was to ensure the song that was his patient's life didn't crescendo in an early and tragic finale.

When he woke, he realized that it was his own heart beating in the machine next to his ear. It echoed through the barren hospital room painted in sterile gray tones. He had been in this room countless times in the past, consulting patients who lay in the very same bed he lay in now. He blinked, eyes focusing on the multiple dots in the ceiling tile.

"Mother Mary's image is in the ceiling tile dots," he said to Dr. Carey, who hurried to his bedside. "Do you suppose that I am having a spiritual vision?"

Carey looked up, reading the pattern that dotted the ceiling like the stars in the night sky. "Do you want me to call the Vatican?"

"We don't want to incite the press. But we should point it out to patients who stay in this room. In fact, we should lie in each bed on this ward, map the constellations and name each room according to what we find. Our patients would like that."

"Consider it done," Carey promised. "How do you feel?"

Noah closed his eyes and took a minute to assess his condition. "Like I have an elephant sitting on my chest," he answered. "But grateful to be alive."

"You should rest. Annie is on her way."

Noah exhaled with a huff. "You called Annie?"

"Your condition is serious." Carey touched his mentor's shoulder.

"I know," Noah's voice dropped to a whisper. "The top cardiothoracic surgeon in the nation laid up in bed with heart failure."

"Your condition doesn't have to be a death sentence. I've scheduled the operating room for tomorrow morning to implant an LVAD device. It will buy you time."

"Carey, I have spent my entire life in the hospital." He pushed himself up, wincing slightly from the pain. He removed his IV, Dfib pads, as well as the multiple heart rate sensors glued to his chest. He knew the risks of open heart surgery. It was a dangerous proposition.

"Dr. Whitley," Carey warned.

"I just need a day." Noah's voice sounded cold in his ears. Realizing the harshness of his tone, he added, "I'll come back tomorrow, and you can cut into me."

"This is against my advisement." Carey supported him as he swung his legs over the side of the bed, placing his feet on the tiled floor.

"Note it in my file." Noah carefully pulled his vanilla cashmere sweater over his head.

"If you feel any nausea, tightness of the chest, or pain in your jaw . . . I want you to come back immediately." Carey assisted his mentor as he stood.

"I know the signs," Noah assured him. He slipped on his pants and shoes.

"What should I tell Annie?" Carey watched as Noah tucked his wallet into his pocket.

"Tell her to meet me at my house in Jersey for dinner at eight o'clock." Noah clasped the gold watch on his wrist.

"Where are you going?" Carey asked.

"I'm going to live. As if this day were my last." Noah put his hand on his student's shoulder.

"Beer and poker or babies and puppies?" Carey asked.

"I'm going to follow my heart, son." He squeezed his shoulder and leaned in to give his prize student a hug. "I'm just going to follow my heart," he repeated softly.

"Please keep your phone with you."

"Of course," Noah promised. "Now, walk an old dying man out for potentially his last day on the planet."

"Yes, sir." Carey walked with Noah down the hallway. "I will take good care of you in there," he promised. "I was taught by the best."

"You are the best," Noah said. "Now it's time for you to prove it." He tried to control the emotion that rose in his throat, threatening to choke him up. The two men hugged at the entrance of the hospital, and Noah walked into the golden rays of the sun on this warm Manhattan spring day.

CHAPTER TEN

Noah walked the busy streets of New York with re-
newed appreciation. He tasted the essence of the Big
Apple as if it were his first and most intoxicating bite.
The bustle, the hustle, the foot traffic that pumped
continuously like blood flowing through veins. He
was awestruck by the vibrancy of the yellow cabs, the
mouthwatering scent of sausage and hotdogs and the
glorious mix of the tragic and ostentatious displayed at
the turn of every corner. The city brimmed with life. It
truly was magical.

What struck him the most were the people. A street
performer played the saxophone with so much passion
that you would have thought his life depended on every
note being played to perfection. The sounds of laughter,
people rushing importantly to and fro, young tourists

snapping candid shots, stretching their limbs in exaggerated poses, men in suits who talked too loudly on mobile phones. Noah was fascinated.

His eyes had been closed to the beauty of this city for more than thirty years. He wondered what could have possibly been so important that it blinded him to this vibrant kaleidoscope of human life.

He knew the answer. He had rushed importantly to and fro while talking loudly on his cellphone, scarcely noticing the people that he walked with. He had been preoccupied with establishing his prominence. Because he wanted so much to matter that nothing else mattered.

He stopped in front of a shop window. Noah's eyes shifted to the reflective surface of the glass, and he saw himself in present time.

The man he saw reflected in the window wasn't happy. He had earned the best that life had to offer, but had lost sight of what was important in the process. Beneath the title, beneath the carefully crafted persona of expertise, he was simply a human being who was born to enjoy the moments that this human life offered. He knew this intuitively when he was young, but had somehow lost his way.

He used to be the kind of man who loved the taste

of tea, who spent hours memorizing every freckle along the surface of his wife's body. He was a man who cried, overwhelmed with joy at the birth of his baby girl. But somehow thirty years had passed without the taste of tea.

He became the type of man who economized, gulping coffee to stay alert. His wife had aged, and he barely noticed. While he was busy soaking up the spotlight, she planned birthday parties, cooked Christmas dinners, drove their daughter to soccer practice and kissed him goodnight before falling asleep. *Had she known? Was she awake and present for the moments of her life? Or had she also fallen into the mindless routine of tasks performed and achievements pursued?* He wished that he could ask her.

Noah's eyes shifted again, looking beneath the plate glass at a poster displayed in the window. The face of an Asian woman in her forties shone through, with pale skin, almond eyes and a delicate smile that hinted at a holy secret. She was purer than any person that Noah had witnessed before, her humanity was completely untouched. It was a strange picture to see displayed in the heart of Manhattan. It looked like it belonged posted on a temple wall in heaven.

Noah's heart took a double beat.

He leaned closer to read the details of the text.

Her name was Suna.

Just one name, like Oprah or Madonna.

Noah had never heard of her before. His eyes scanned the next line of text.

She was giving a lecture on the *spiritual significance of life* and this was her twelve hundredth lecture on something called the ChunBuKyung, which was an ancient numerical codex from South Korea that mapped the origin and completion of the soul.

He checked his watch. The lecture had begun twenty minutes ago.

He opened the door to the hotel where her picture was displayed, grabbed a pamphlet on the lecture and made his way to the convention room where the event was located.

When he entered the auditorium, he found a place to stand behind the last row of seats in the room where approximately three hundred people sat in attendance.

At the front of the room sat the Korean woman whose picture had captured Noah's attention in the window. She was everything her portrait professed. She was pure but had depth. A person could live a thousand years and not possess the untold galaxies of wisdom that shone from her eyes. Her dark hair was fashioned in a chignon, and she wore a conservative dress made of fine ivory silk that buttoned up to her neck and fell to the floor. She rang a single brass bell between delicate fingers that glimmered in the stage lights and twinkled like the North Star.

Noah was transfixed.

Her voice carried through the auditorium with a full-bodied softness that swaddled each person as if every particle of ether were a tiny speaker cooing the ancient secret of the original mother directly into their ears.

"Actually, the ChunBuKyung was never meant to be a secret," she said. "In the beginning of time, the ChunBuKyung was so obvious that it wasn't necessary for it to be recorded on stone, parchment or paper. We knew what it was simply because our lives were infused within its wordless essence.

"But since we have ceased to perceive life from this original state of mind, it is difficult to understand that everything on the Earth, every particle of heaven, every atom in the human body is intimately connected as one at the foundation of reality. Until you feel it in your own body you will never get it." She smiled. "And that is why I am here. Today you will understand the essence of the ChunBuKyung without me decoding it character by character, because you will feel it for yourself."

She smiled, turning her attention to someone in the front row of the auditorium. "Everything is made of energy. You, me, the plant on this table, this bell. Everything is made of the energy of God but each thing expresses a unique chord of vibration that creates the illusion of difference. Nonetheless, at its very foundation it's all the same, the one unchangeable essence of God."

A powerful wave of heat overcame Noah, a tidal wave that crashed down from all sides. A sheen of sweat instantly manifested along the entire length of his body. He grabbed the chair that he stood behind for support. He couldn't comprehend the breathless sensation of drowning that kept his lungs from taking a full inhalation. His lungs merely puffed within his ribcage like balloons as he took his breath in short gasps.

As abruptly as this stifling heat swept over him, it passed.

He could breathe again.

He exhaled with a long sigh and drew a smooth breath in.

He felt like he was floating. Like a baby drifting in a warm bath. He overflowed with the sensation of pure undiluted life.

The auditorium seemed to glimmer. Light shone around every object as if it were simply a holograph.

He rubbed his eyes.

Who is this woman?

As the thought passed through his mind, the woman at the front of the room paused, mid-sentence, turning her head quickly as if she had heard her name called. They locked eyes, and she spoke directly to him.

"From the foundational essence, all life is birthed into an unending kaleidoscope of forms. You are a beautiful life contained within that kaleidoscope. And just as the images of a kaleidoscope change, so do the many faces and forms of our world. But at the very foundation it's all God. We are made from God, of God, existing in God."

She broke eye contact with Noah, looked at another person in the audience and spoke gently, "Our species knew this intuitively at our origin. When this knowledge became obsolete, the ChunBuKyung was recorded and kept hidden through the dark ages in order to protect it from being destroyed by the religions and governments that would have sought to eliminate this knowledge at all costs.

"There is no other. We are one and the same. We are Self, experiencing itself in a myriad of forms. That is the message of the ChunBuKyung. It has been passed down through the ages at great risk to the bearers of this text so that one day this message could come to you. It is a spiritual map that will guide you back to our original state of being."

Suna stood at the front of the auditorium, the hem of her ivory dress brushing the ground as she walked across the stage. "I will introduce this text so that you may experience it for yourself. After all, experience is the best teacher." She smiled. "But before I share it with you, I would like to start with an exercise so that you may practice opening your senses to fully perceive the essence of the ChunBuKyung."

She raised the brass bell between her fingertips and rang it once.

"Close your eyes and listen to the sound of the bell with your ears."

Noah closed his eyes. The tinkle of the bell was high and soft.

"Now practice feeling the vibration of the sound in your body." She rang it again.

Noah felt a small sensation in his body. The high ting of the bell stimulated his nerve endings, which caused the hairs along the surface of his body to rise.

"Now that you have distinguished the difference

between listening with your ears versus perceiving with your whole body, I will chant the ChunBuKyung once for you. The vibrational essence of each sound will be absorbed into your body, which will allow your body to recover its memory of origin on a cellular level. You don't have to *do* anything, you just have to bring your awareness to the present and the energetic resonance will recalibrate you to a pure state of being. It only takes a split second of presence for your soul to open completely."

Suna nodded her head to the sound engineer who raised the volume on a tribal music track. The melodic beat of the drum echoed through the room. Suna began to chant, softly at first, raising the intensity of her voice with every character uttered,

"Il. Shi. Mu. Shi. Il. Suk. Sahm. Geuk. Mu. Jin. Bohn.
Chun. Il. Il. Ji. Il. Yi. In. Il. Sahm.
Il. Juk. Ship. Guh. Mu. Gwe. Hwa. Sahm.
Chun. Yi. Sahm. Ji. Yi. Sahm. In. Yi. Sahm.
Dae. Sahm. Hap. Yook. Saeng. Chil. Pahl. Gu. Woon.
Sahm. Sah. Sung. Hwan. Oh. Chil. Il.
Myo. Yun. Mahn. Wang. Mahn. Rhae.
Yong. Byun. Bu. Dong. Bohn.
Bohn. Shim. Bohn. Tae. Yahng. Ahng. Myung.
In. Joong. Chun. Ji. Il. Il. Jong. Mu. Jong. Il."

Noah closed his eyes and allowed his body to absorb the rhythm of the drum and the energy that the chanted words pulled from the ether and channeled into the room.

He experienced something that he wouldn't be able to explain, even if he tried. A holy fire emerged from deep within. His soul expanded, like a golden dragon rising from a thousand-year suppression to spread its wings majestically through his limbs. It relived each moment of his life, every breath he had taken, every drop of sweat, every tension, every love gained and lost.

In this moment, he was *known*.

"God?" he breathed, attempting to identify this glorious light.

"Yes." Suna's voice echoed through his head, communicated impossibly without words.

He opened his eyes and met her gaze, which had been intently fixed on him without faltering. She nodded her head, a glimmer of moisture sparkling in her eyes. He knew, that she knew, that something important had just happened for him.

CHAPTER ELEVEN

Before Noah had the chance to form a coherent thought, the event had concluded and he was whisked into Suna's greenroom, per her request, by her personal liaison. Two possibilities occurred to him. The first, and the less likely, was that she had also witnessed the golden dragon leaping from his chest. The second, and far more likely scenario, was that he had imagined the whole thing, and she had merely called the old doctor to her greenroom to make sure he didn't need psychiatric care after watching him spread his arms to reenact a mythical creature in flight, like a total nutcase. Whatever the reason, he was nervous to meet her.

He jumped reflexively when the door to the green room opened. When Suna entered the room, a look of pure delight crossed her features. She offered both of her hands to Noah, squeezed his palms once and crinkled her eyes with affection.

"How did you find me?" she asked with a certain air of familiarity, as if the two of them had been reunited after the end of a very long game of hide-and-seek.

"I saw your poster in the window," he answered dumbly.

"I was afraid that you weren't going to come."

"You were expecting me?"

"Of course," she answered simply. She was light-hearted, congenial and quick to laugh. She was nothing like what Noah had expected. She sat on the edge of the coffee table and invited him to take a seat on her dressing chair. "Tell me about yourself?"

"What would you like to know?"

"What's your name?"

"Noah," he said.

"Have you had a good life?" She tilted her head slightly and looked into his eyes with open sincerity.

He paused, unsure how to answer that question. It was a little too straightforward for his liking. Three weeks ago, he would have asserted that he was happy. He would have told her about the awards that he had displayed on his office walls, his humanitarian efforts, and he would have proudly shared the details of his family life and boasted of his daughter who was soon to be married. But today, he wasn't sure if he'd been happy at all. If he had been, he was too busy to enjoy more than a moment or two of this contentment.

He shifted uncomfortably in his chair. "I'd be a lot happier if I could live until my daughter's wedding," he answered, surprised by his frankness.

"Are you ill?" She leaned forward and touched his knee with genteel concern.

"Yes," he confessed.

"Is it your heart?"

"How do you know that?"

"Your blood. It smells dense."

"You can smell my blood?"

"My senses are acute," she explained. "You just need to improve your circulation."

"I'm pretty sure that I need a lot more than that." He knew that a few minutes of calisthenics wouldn't change anything.

"You really don't," she assured him gently.

"I know precisely the implications of my condition." Her light assurance irked him. "I'm a heart specialist." he added, tempering the undertone of superiority in his voice.

"So am I." Her eyes flashed with finality.

Something inside of him told him that he was out-ranked. "Perhaps experts on different ends of the spectrum?" he said, deciding to pose a compromise.

"Perhaps," she conceded. "I know someone who can help you. Without doctors, without hospitals, without machines and wires implanted in your chest."

"Who?" Noah was intrigued.

She stood, stepping past him to reach for a small photo frame on her dressing table. It was a snapshot of her standing with an elderly Native American gentleman, whose hair was as white as snow. The duo looked happy in hiking gear posed in front of a red stone mountain, obviously located in the Southwest region of the United States.

She handed the frame to Noah, who examined the details of the man's face. Though he was obviously in his sixties, his face was fresh and youthful. Also, he seemed familiar, though Noah was certain they'd never met. While he studied the portrait, he unconsciously thumbed the pendant tucked beneath his vanilla cashmere sweater.

His mind drifted to the memory of the Native grandmother who had given him the crystal in exchange for medical services over thirty years ago. He had tried to refuse the gift, explaining that his work on the reservation was pro bono, free of charge, but she insisted that the pendant belonged to him, promising that it would bring him great power when he needed it most. He wondered if the man in the photo was from the same tribe as the Native woman.

"His name is K'ete-t," she said. "When I was a young girl learning the principles of the ChunBuKyung, he told me that I would grow into a great Tao Master who would share its principles with the world. On the day that this photo was taken, he predicted that during my twelve hundredth lecture I would meet a kindred spirit." She returned the photo to the table. "It's you, Noah."

"I don't think that . . ." Noah looked up, uncertain of what to make of this information.

"I recognize this," she interrupted him, leaning forward to touch the pendant around his neck. "What does it mean to you?"

The necklace that she recognized was the one given to him by the Native grandmother. "I wear it to remind me why I went into medicine."

"And why did you go into medicine?" Her keen eyes flashed.

"To help people."

"Exactly." She smiled. "But your destiny is perhaps greater than you imagined." The intensity of her stare increased. "K'ete-t is waiting for you in Sedona. Have you heard of it?"

"In Arizona?" he asked, turning to scan the background of the photo on the table. It appeared to be one and the same.

"If you go there, your heart will be healed," she promised. "And if you meet this man, you will discover the greater purpose for your life." She pointed to the man in the photo frame. "The choice is yours," she said, as if it was a decision he had made long ago.

CHAPTER TWELVE

"Spar?" Quauhtli asked with a mischievous glint in his eye. They had concluded their tour of the estate with the martial arts training studio.

Carlos whistled. "I think he's serious."

"You know that I could never take you, Father," Leuters said.

"Try." His father's face crinkled with a smile.

"Prepare to watch me be defeated, Carlos." Leuters slapped him on the back as he stepped into the arena.

"I'd like to see that." Carlos scrutinized the father/son duo. They were about as well matched as the Jolly Green Giant and Jiminy Cricket.

"Trust me. It won't take long," Leuters promised. He met his father on the mat and offered a half bow. The two men began to spar. Leuters's father had slowed

with age but was able to anticipate his son's combat tac-
tics as if he could read his mind.

"Was there something that you wanted to ask
me?" His father spoke effortlessly while dodging
Leuters's strikes.

"I have a choice to make." Leuters's kick caught
nothing but air.

"And what is this choice?" Quauhtli stepped to
the side.

"I have discovered a medicine that will help many
people. But it's been made illegal." His kick landed in
the center of his father's palm.

"According to who?" Quauhtli grabbed his son's foot
and used the momentum to pull him off balance, sending Leuters to the floor.

"The law." He jumped back up to his feet.

"Whose law?" His father crouched and pivoted his
body in a leg sweep.

"The governmental law." Leuters jumped.

"You say that this medicine will help people?"
Quauhtli blocked a punch with his forearm. The
two men performed a rapid succession of blows and
counter strikes.

"Very much."

"Then you must continue."

"If I am caught, the repercussions will be devastating."

"Then don't get caught."

"I am frightened."

"Then you will be caught." His father tapped an acupressure point lightly in Leuters's rib cage, and he fell to the ground. His father stood above him. "I cannot advise you to walk away and spend your life in a safe state of regret. Nor can I tell you to run head first into controversy for the sake of goodness. You ask me a question that only you can answer." He pulled his son to his feet and bowed. "But there is something that I can give you."

"What is it, Father?" Leuters returned the bow.

"Your inheritance." His father opened a weapons chest and pulled out a bronze sword. "Carlos, will you excuse us for a moment?" He addressed Carlos for the first time since their introduction. "I have a message to deliver to my son."

***

"What did he say?" Carlos asked, shifting the car into gear.

Leuters had been silent for over an hour. Carlos had respectfully allowed him space to think. He had gone to see his father for answers, but left with more questions. Whatever step he took next would unalterably change the trajectory of his life. It was a weighted decision.

"I vowed to never reveal the message." Leuters looked out the window.

"What was the sword for?" Carlos questioned.

"To give me power."

"Power for what?"

"To accomplish my mission."

"To manufacture MFS?

"To follow my destiny."

"Does that destiny include MFS?" Carlos held his breath while he waited for the answer. Leuters noticed that his body stiffened in his seat. Something seemed off.

"If I choose," Leuters answered carefully.

"Have you chosen?"

"Yes. I have chosen, yes."

"You are doing the right thing." Carlos exhaled, and his body relaxed. He pulled the car into a gas station. "I have to make a phone call to prepare for our arrival."

"I don't know if I'll be up for a community meeting just yet," Leuters said, exhaling. "I have only just decided. I'm not quite ready to celebrate taking on the SSA as an opponent."

"Not a community meeting," Carlos assured him.

"Just a meeting with a financier."

"Very well," Leuters conceded. "Make the call."

CHAPTER THIRTEEN

"Are you coming?" Leuters reached over the passenger seat of the car to grab his satchel.

"I'll be there in a minute." Carlos held his phone in the air and examined the screen. "I'm just going to call the financiers and find out how far off they are." He moved the phone through the air, looking for a signal. "I'm right behind you."

Leuters hoisted the satchel over his shoulder and balanced the bronze sword precariously on his leg as he unlocked the front door to his *casa*. When he stepped into the empty house, his nose was hit with the pungent smell of dirt. It smelled wet, like potting soil.

"What in the . . . ?" The odor came from the living room, and the couch seemed to be the source of the overpowering scent. He lifted the dust skirt to investigate. It took a few seconds to comprehend what he saw: multiple bags of fertilizer and plastic bottles filled with clear liquid that were connected by bundles of wires that routed to a stopwatch.

"Bomb!" he yelled. "Carlos, bomb!"

The countdown clock flipped to display the number three. Leuters turned and ran toward the door. He felt the heat on his back before he heard the sound of the explosion. The impact lifted him into the air and carried him out the door as if he were a bird in flight. He felt the hot sting of metal followed by the crash of his body against the unforgiving ground. And then he felt nothing at all.

***

The beep of the heart monitor. The sound of oxygen released from a metallic tank in rhythmic spurts. The quiet murmur of voices. The clink of the clipboard against the metal bedframe. Leuters was suspended in an eternity of these sounds. Time and space had no meaning.

It took all of his might to open his eyes. He didn't know how long he had been unconscious. A nurse in the room sensed him stir and rushed to his bedside. She rubbed his shoulder and shushed him. She was a pretty Hispanic girl who wore too much makeup.

"You are in the hospital," she said. "There was an accident."

It all came rushing back.

Africa. MFS. The pharmaceutical rep.

Prison. His father. The bronze sword. The mission.

And finally, the bomb.

"Carlos?" he slurred, attempting to push himself on his elbows.

"Shhh." She lightly pushed him back to the pillow. "He's just fine. He has been here to see you every day. He will come again tonight."

Leuters was grateful that Carlos had stayed outside to make a phone call. He wouldn't have been able to live with himself if any harm had come to his friend.

"I'm going to get the doctor." The nurse tucked the sheets tightly around him. "You stay right here."

Leuters nodded. He was too weak to go anywhere, anyway. The haze of heavy narcotics draped over him like a wet blanket. He closed his eyes and floated in a thoughtless state of nothingness.

"Mr. Garcia?" A gentleman's voice pulled him from his drug-induced meditation.

He opened his eyes. A man in his thirties who wore blue scrubs and a white lab coat stood by his bed. He looked at the clipboard in his hand and examined the medical chart.

"Do you know where you are?"

Leuters nodded.

"My name is Dr. Lopez."

Leuters nodded again. It was difficult to speak under the veil of the medication.

"Do you remember what happened?" Dr. Lopez asked.

"Explosion," Leuters answered in a hoarse whisper.

"That is correct," the doctor confirmed. "I have some difficult news."

"I'm a doctor," Leuters explained. "I am familiar with the terminology. Do I have internal injuries?"

"A few broken ribs."

Leuters exhaled. A few broken ribs he could deal with.

The doctor placed his hand on Leuters's arm. "There's more. You lost your right leg. The sword you were carrying when the bomb went off severed your leg when you landed. We did everything that we could. I'm sorry."

"I don't have a leg?" His voice rose an octave.

"I'm sorry, Dr. Garcia. There was nothing we could do. However, with rehabilitation and the use of pros-thetics, you will be able to walk again."

"Without a leg?" he moaned.

"With the use of prosthetics."

Leuters wept openly. A flash of images played through his mind. He saw all of the things that he would never do again: run down the beach feeling the wet sand break between his toes, walk barefoot in the wet green grass, pick up discarded socks and under-wear from the ground when he was too lazy to bend over. Jogging, walking, skiing, swimming. Nothing would be the same again.

"I would rather have lost anything else: a kidney, a lung, an eye." His head dropped to the pillow, and the hot tears that flowed down the side of his face dripped onto the pillowcase. He wouldn't be able to dance with his wife at their wedding or wrap his feet around hers when they made love. He hadn't met her yet, but he had dreamed of her since he was a boy. His mind flashed the image of him making love with only one leg.

It broke his heart.

"I rather would have died."

"I know it is a shock," Dr. Lopez said compassion-ately. "I assure you, you can lead a relatively normal life."

Leuters had taken his legs for granted. They were *his*. A part of him. He owned them. And someone took them away.

"Who did this to me?" Anger rose up his spine, a fire

from deep in his core.

"The police have no suspects," the doctor said quietly.

"I must talk to Carlos," he stated, determined.

"We have called him. He will be here soon," the doctor assured him. "Can I get anything for you? How is the pain?"

"Tolerable," Leuters's answered resolutely.

His single-sighted focus was on discovering who did this to him and exacting revenge.

"Dr. Garcia," the doctor said as he put his hand on his shoulder. "This is a lot to take in. You can expect to experience the various stages of grief. Just allow yourself to move through them. There is no wrong way to feel. Your life will change, but you can live a happy and productive life with a few minor adjustments. We have arranged an appointment with the hospital therapist to help you process what you may be feeling in these initial stages."

"I am only feeling one thing right now," Leuters said evenly. "Vengeance."

CHAPTER FOURTEEN

"Papa." Annie rushed outside to greet her father when he stepped onto the stoop of their New Jersey family estate. She folded her arms around him and cozied her head deep into his chest.

Noah brushed her curls aside and kissed her forehead. "Are you ready to make dinner? Why don't we make your mama's pasta?"

She raised her tear-stained eyes and nodded. This reminded him of the time that she met him on this very porch when she was ten years old, after mustering all of her bravery to confess that she'd broken the wheel on his model car while using it to chauffeur her Barbie doll around the house, even though he had asked her not to. He'd been so moved by her trembling courage that he comforted her instead of punishing her. The years had passed, she had grown into a woman, but to him she would always be that little girl.

Annie brushed the tears from her cheeks and stepped into the house.

Noah closed the front door behind them. "Did Carey fill you in?"

"Yes," she said. "But if you are having surgery tomorrow, we shouldn't be eating, right?" She furrowed her brow, having just comprehended this contradictory detail.

"I'm not going to have surgery tomorrow." He draped his arm over her shoulder and led her into the kitchen that had scarcely been used since her mother's death. The room was still as cheerful as she had left it, with its bright yellow walls and accents of red. It was a happy kitchen filled with memories of happier times. Noah felt his wife's absence the most while standing in this room. That's why he avoided it.

Annie leaned her elbows on the butcher block island. "I don't understand. Whatever's on your schedule can wait. There's nothing more important than having this surgery. This is your *life*, Dad."

"It's not a scheduling issue." He pulled a massive pot from an overhead cabinet and placed it in the sink to fill it with water. "I'm not having the surgery, ever."

"Dad," she growled, readying herself for the fight of the century.

Noah knew from thirty years of experience the battle of wills that was about to unfold in this kitchen, and it was admittedly amusing for him to witness his own sense of determination reflected in his daughter's defiant stance. Nevertheless, he also knew that he would be the victor.

"You are your father's daughter," he chastised affectionately.

"You are having that surgery," she commanded.

"I'm not scared of you," he laughed.

"You should be."

"I'm going to Sedona."

"No."

"Yes."

"Dad."

"Daughter."

"Think about it," she reasoned. "You're a surgeon . . . you *know* the risks."

"I have thought about it," he explained. "And I am taking a calculated risk."

"What's in Sedona?" she huffed, insolently.

"I'm not sure. Something, maybe."

"It doesn't make sense." She scrubbed her face with

her palms in frustration. She was moments away from stomping her feet.

"I know. It doesn't have to make sense."

CHAPTER FIFTEEN

Noah walked barefoot across the room, wearing only his boxer shorts, and swept the curtains that covered the picture window aside. His toothbrush almost fell out of his mouth when he saw the crimson rays of sunrise stream through an unending range of red rocks. They seemed to wrap around his hotel as far as the eye could see, almost too magnificent to fully take in at once. He was grateful that his travel agent booked a flight that arrived after nightfall, which had enabled this sudden and dramatic unveiling of the early morning Sedona landscape. He couldn't have planned it better if he had tried.

Noah found it most effective to eye the landscape in sections, in order to fully appreciate the details of this picturesque scene. He understood how Sedona got its reputation for being a mystical land. The rock formations were so extraordinary that the witnessing of them made anything seem possible. Even the sight of a unicorn outside of his window wouldn't have surprised him while in such a state of awe.

His examination concluded only when he ran out of window. He turned away from the view to resume his morning routine and paused, turning to look outside once more. One rock in particular caught his eye. He laughed and sat on the bed in half-lotus to mimic the upright posture of the rock.

"Even the rocks in Sedona meditate," he chuckled, brushing his teeth.

**

Noah explored the quiet mountain town in his rented luxury SUV. Every turn of the single lane highway brought an exciting new sight as his car slowly wove through the mountains on the south side of the city. A single mountain in the shape of a bell stood apart from the neighboring buttes.

Suna's voice echoed through his head. *Go up Bell Rock and you will find your answer.* Remembering their encounter calmed him. Something about her presence reminded him of home. Not the home that he grew up in, not even the home that he had created with his wife and daughter, but an unnamed home that existed long before. This intuitive sense of knowing was impossible to quantify. That instinct compelled him to listen to the message echoing through his thoughts.

Bell Rock's depth of color was marvelous; its red hue was much deeper than that of the neighboring buttes. Its porous texture was also unique, like refined lava. Noah sensed there was something special about the land. The higher the path led, the steeper the incline became. Scaling the mountain was physically strenuous, and the steep drop to the ground added another whole layer of psychological difficulty. Even so, he was determined to climb as far as he could. Approximately twenty feet from the top, he stopped to catch his breath, sitting next to an old juniper tree.

"This is close enough," he said aloud, figuring that any healing energy that existed at the top of the butte could reach him here. He was close.

Go to the top. A voice echoed through his head, clearer than any thought he'd ever had before. It wasn't his voice, but Suna's. Noah looked behind him to assess the steep climb. He closed his eyes again, certain that he had gone far enough. *Go to the top.* The message rang through his mind. Noah took a minute to contemplate whether this was a spiritual message or just a random thought emerging from his subconscious. If the heavens wanted to give him a message, shouldn't it come from a loud voice of authority booming from the sky or perhaps a burning bush?

Go to the top, NOW! Suna's voice boomed from one side of his brain to the other.

"Okay," Noah said aloud. "Looks like I'm going to the top." He assessed the almost imperceptible footholds and sighed in resignation. "Well, I'm gonna die anyway."

One by one, he found the holds and pulled himself up. His heartbeat echoed loudly in his ears. He heaved his body over the final ridge and reached the uppermost landing.

"I made it," he breathed. He maneuvered himself to a sitting position in order to scan the view from the top of the mountain. He took a long, triumphant breath in and exhaled. There was a profound stillness, a type of hyperreality that surrounded him. It wasn't like a dream. There was nothing fuzzy about his perception; he was clearly aware of every aspect of reality with a type of nanoperception. He could feel everything.

He sensed the particles of the sun descend slowly through the air. A soft breeze tickled every hair along his body. The moist richness of the red rock beneath him seemed more like a sponge than a rock. There was nothing hard or stationary about it. It was alive, moving subtly with the breath of life. He sat in half-lotus facing east, but he could see the landscape of Sedona 360 degrees around him. Impossibly, he felt the 360 degrees of Sedona observe him. He understood the message that had been relayed a thousand times from the various saints and sages throughout the ages.

"I am . . ." His thought was interrupted by a small vibration from the rock beneath his seat. The Earth trembled, a precursor to his life being changed forever.

CHAPTER SIXTEEN

Dual swirls of light—copper and mauve—twisted like twirling ribbons as they rose from the Earth. They spiraled around Noah in a double helix, like strands of cosmic DNA. Effervescent gold particles spurted from the Earth, rising in a golden tidal wave that gently lifted his soul from his body and carried it into the silver-blue particles of the sky, stretching the astral cord that connected his body to his soul like a rubber band.

Is this real? He looked down and saw his body seated in half-lotus. *Did I fall asleep and not realize it?*

His perception flew high in the Sedona sky, suspending him in a moment of pure bliss. The particles of heaven and Earth danced between the particles of his soul as he drifted in the sky. The light reweaved through the tapestry of his existence in a holy recreation of being.

The ribbons of light that had that propelled his soul upward began to spin at top speed. They created a vortex that instantly towed his soul deep into the womb of the Earth, located beneath Bell Rock. He landed in a vast cavern, thirty feet high and supported by six massive aquamarine pillars. Precious stones and geodes, crystals shaped exactly like the landscapes of Sedona, created a tiny model town that glittered all the colors of the rainbow.

At the very center of the room—between the four-foot high crimson Bell Rock carved from a single block of ruby, the diamond Cathedral Rock that sparkled like a crystalline altar, and the emerald Airport Mesa— stood a quartz pedestal that displayed a crystal orb. Noah looked inside the crystal ball, wondering if he would see his future, as he had heard was possible in many folk tales.

I must be dreaming.

He did not find his future inside the crystal ball. Instead, he saw an opaque stone, the whitest of whites, that resembled a human brain. Numerous pillars of deep blue-green aquamarine sprung from the stone.

The air pressure in the room shifted. A feminine spirit materialized before his eyes. Her aqua eyes were a striking contrast to skin that glowed with the radiance of Sedona's copper rocks. Long dark hair fell in gentle waves that glistened like the wings of a raven, and her transparent robes of white, accented with touches of turquoise, overlapped the crystal pedestal. The crystal ball that contained the aquamarine occupied the space of her heart.

"Hwanggung," she whispered in greeting. When she spoke, the aquamarine came to life, illuminating the room with a soft blue glow.

"Hwanggung," Noah repeated, as if he were John Smith attempting to communicate with Pocahontas in her native tongue.

The woman laughed, aqua light surging so brightly that Noah had to shield his eyes.

"You misunderstand," she corrected. "Your name is Hwanggung."

"You speak English?"

"I speak all the languages of the Earth," she said. "I see that you've received my gift." She indicated the crystal tied around his neck, given to him by the Native grandmother. He held the pendant between his fingers.

"Who are you?" he asked.

"My name is Mago. I am your mother."

"I'm sorry, but I don't understand."

She smiled.

Noah was mesmerized by her haunting beauty.

"Throughout time, many people have called me by many names. I am the Mother of the Earth. And you are Hwanggung. That is what I named you when I created you at the beginning of time," she explained. "Your life has gone on, you have had many faces and names, but you have always been, and will ever be, my eldest son. I have waited for this moment for a very long time. I knew that you would come." Her eyes glimmered with unabashed affection.

"You knew that I would come?" he asked. "How?"

"Because you made a promise to me."

"I don't remember."

"You will." She smiled. "When our souls meet, you will remember." She reached her hands forward and stroked between Noah's brows with her thumbs, as if dusting grime from the face of a child. His vision cleared; everything in the room became brighter. When he looked into the crystal ball within her chest, his soul was reflected upon its surface. It was shrouded in darkness.

His face was covered in darkness and twisted grotesquely. "I look like a monster."

"This world has left its scars on you," she said. "I will help you. But you have to let go."

"I can't," he protested. He was horrified—overwhelmed with a profound sense of unworthiness.

"It's all right," she said. "You are a good man. The illness you see is a temporary condition created by the world you've lived in. A long time ago, you promised to return to the Earth when humanity was on the precipice of change. You are a leader. I need your help, but we don't have much time. In order for you to help me, you must first let me help you." The aqua light in her soul surged and a layer of darkness was pulled from the image of Noah's soul projected on the surface of the crystal ball.

When the first layer of darkness was lifted from the image, it was also erased from his body. One after another, they both experienced every persona that he had created for survival. A flash of monstrous images that seemed to never end were extracted from his field of consciousness, and the weight of his ego was released, layer by layer, in a continuous process of surrender that was incredibly intimate. These images flew into Mago's soul so quickly that Noah's head felt like it might burst from the pressure of their release. But, beneath the pain, he felt the light of his soul again, for the first time in ages.

He had thought that he was a good man, but he realized that, beneath the carefully crafted personas, he was filled with war, manipulation, and hate. She received the poisons that he had carried for so long directly into the light of her soul, without judgment, without filter. There was no pretending. She saw everything.

The final layer was the most difficult to release. When it was pulled from him, he felt a contraction in his chest. He gagged and a rank gas released into the room, followed by an explosion of heat in his chest that took his breath away.

She cried, having just intimately felt every morsel of the pain that his soul had endured, as if it were her own. Noah also cried, but for very different reasons. She took his pain. She left love in its wake. That was the incredible heart of his mother. The pendant around his neck shone, the colors of the rainbow glistening in a clear ascending line.

"Hwanggung," she said softly.

"I remember," he cried.

"Do you know what you must do?"

"Yes, Mother. I have seen them all." The faces of his three siblings, who had also vowed to come back at this time, shone as clear as day within the spaces of his mind.

"You must gather them here."

"I only know Suna."

"I have called the other two. Look for them."

"I will," he promised. He would find them, and they

would fulfill their mission. The world would change for the better. It was their destiny, simply because it was a choice they had made long ago.

CHAPTER SEVENTEEN

Carlos helped Leuters rise from the seat of the car. This was his first time home since being admitted to the hospital. But it wasn't his home that he'd returned to, it was Carlos's. Leuters's home no longer existed. Leuters took a deep breath in when he stood, holding onto the car for support.

"You got it?" Carlos asked as he rushed to his side attentively.

"My first step without assistance in nine months," Leuters said. "I'm ready."

He took a wobbly step forward, followed by another. By the time he reached the front door, his stride had more confidence.

"You're doing good, man," Carlos encouraged.

Leuters cast a sideways glance. He knew that Carlos

was being supportive, but Leuters didn't appreciate the encouragement. He had spent a lifetime being strong, and needing any kind of support made him feel vulnerable. The rehabilitation process was humbling, and he was ready to put it behind him.

"Of course I am doing well," he said, trying to temper his voice. "I have had six months of practice."

"Okay, well, you let me know if you need anything," Carlos said. "I have you set up in my old office. Maria made a bed for you." Carlos unlocked the door.

"I will only be here a few months, until I get back on my feet again." Leuters laughed, "Literally."

"You can stay as long as you need." Carlos led him to the makeshift bedroom. A single mattress with floral bedding was set up amid the workout equipment and computer desk. Beside the bed was the bronze sword. Leuters's heart stopped when he saw it. His inheritance. The maker of his destiny. He looked at his artificial foot.

"What is that doing here?" he asked angrily, motioning toward the sword.

Carlos shifted uncomfortably. "I wasn't sure if you wanted it or not," he said, moving quickly to retrieve it and take it out of the room.

"Wait," Leuters called him back.

Carlos returned with the sword.

"I can't let my fear control me," Leuters said, holding his hands out. "Please give it to me."

Carlos put the sword into Leuters's open palms.

The moment the smoke-stained bronze touched his flesh, Leuters was pulled into another reality. He saw himself standing on a red rock mountain, slicing the air majestically. His body swayed with the power of a warrior and the grace of a poet. This sword was a part of him. More now than ever. This vision was a call to action.

"Leuters?" Carlos asked. *Is he okay?*

Leuters heard his name filter through his ears. At the same time, he heard the question echo through his head. "What?" He snapped his head up.

"Are you okay?" Carlos asked.

"Yeah." Leuters shook his head. "I'm fine."

"Maybe you should rest?" Carlos suggested.

"Yeah." He sat on the bed, holding the sword across his thighs.

"I'm sorry about your leg," Carlos apologized. *You were supposed to die.*

"What?" Leuters's head shot up.

"I said that I am sorry about your leg." *You were supposed to die.*

"*Amigo*, I might be going crazy, but did you say that . . ."

I hate you.

Leuters shook his head. "*Amigo*, did I do something to offend you?"

"What are you talking about?" Carlos smiled.

"Did I do anything to hurt you?" Leuters asked.

You abandoned me. "No," Carlos answered easily.

"If I did, I am sorry," he apologized.

You left me all by myself. And now you will pay.

"Carlos?"

It was me who sent you to prison. It was me who arranged the bomb. I am the informant. "Yes?" Carlos smiled.

Leuters looked at the bronze sword in his lap. "My inheritance."

"What?" Carlos asked.

"I became one with the sword. It cut off my leg. It is a part of me now," Leuters breathed.

"What are you talking about?"

"I treated you like a brother."

You are my brother.

"I know." Leuters was shocked at Carlos's unconscious confession. Now that he had been reunited with the sword, he could hear Carlos's thoughts. He had cried for his brother, not knowing that he had been by his side for years, pretending to be a friend while plotting his revenge.

"Know what?" Carlos was confused.

"Why would you do this to me?" Leuters's voice caught in his throat.

Vengeance. "Do what?" Carlos asked innocently.

"I have to go." Leuters stood abruptly. "This was a mistake."

"*Amigo.*" Carlos tried to stop him.

"Let me go, Carlos. Before this turns ugly."

"What is the matter?" Carlos asked as he followed him through the house.

"You framed me." Leuters strode out the front door angrily.

Carlos was stunned. He looked like he had been hit with a ton of bricks. "No, I didn't." *How does he know?*

"Don't lie to me."

"I'm not lying."

"Alexandro." Leuters called his brother by his true name.

The disingenuous smile was wiped from Carlos's face. He looked around. A few of the neighbors had paused their activities to watch the confrontation.

"Why?" Leuters asked, his voice pained. "All I was

doing was trying to help the world."

"Because you never tried to help me."

"I couldn't find you."

"You and your rich father looked for me once, maybe twice, in ten years? You lived in a palace like a prince, and you left me on the streets like a rat." His voice shook with rage. "That is why, *brother*." He spit the word from his lips like it was poison.

"Did you send me to prison?"

"The SSA sent you to prison."

"Did you plant the bomb?"

"The pharmaceutical company set the bomb."

"Did you alert them?" Leuters asked desperately.

"I only told them the truth," he hissed. "And I swear to you, *brother* . . . I will spend the rest of my life ensuring that you suffer as I have!" he yelled, as Leuters turned and limped down the street.

CHAPTER EIGHTEEN

"When the sky is lit with starry light, I kiss the moon and say goodnight." Angeline spoke her line wistfully. She twirled in the moonlight, and the ribbons sewn into her costume created a magnificent satin cage around her. "I must go to see the temptress that we all know. And if by morning I shall die, at least I would have bid my last goodbye."

She stepped daintily across the stage lighted by torchlight, constructed in the local park. The whir of applause sent a chill through her body. The stage was the only place where she felt comfortable: wearing someone else's clothes, speaking someone else's words, losing herself in someone else's life. It was the place where she was freed of everything "Angeline"—all of her thoughts, her problems and her so-called gifts.

She loved to play pretend.

But it wasn't just pretend. When she acted, she was making a wish with all of her body to be somebody, anybody, but her.

Out of the corner of her eye, she caught sight of the production assistant staring at her with critical distain. She knew from previous experience what would come once the curtain was drawn.

"Angeline. I need to talk to you."

"Of course. How can I help you?"

"You missed three shows last week. We have decided to go in another direction. Tonight will be your last performance with the company. We hope that you understand."

"Of course. I'm sorry to have put you in this position. I am sure that it was difficult to replace me on those nights. Again, I'm truly sorry and please thank the director for the opportunity."

Then she collects her things and disappears into the night. This was a script that she had enacted too many times in the past. She wished for a new script.

***

"Well, that's a disappointment, darling," her mother cooed disingenuously through the telephone line. "But you're too good for them anyway. It was just a local theatre production."

"Mom," Angeline said. "It wasn't just a local production in a park. I loved the character, I loved the lines and I loved the show. It was magical," she said, scooping another handful of popcorn into her mouth.

"But, darling, you have been on *television*," her mother said, as if this held some great importance. "You need to focus on taking steps forward, not backward."

"A guest spot on a pilot hardly makes me a television star. Besides, I need the work."

What she really meant was that she needed the money.

"You just need some rest, sweetie. Do you have any valium?" her mother asked.

"You're not helping."

"I'm trying."

"Thanks."

They both paused awkwardly. The more years they spent living their separate lives, the more difficulty they had making a solid connection. But they still tried, out of respect for the institution of the mother/daughter relationship.

"Have you talked to your father recently?"

"He's doing pretty well," Angeline said, thinking to add, "He misses you."

"Well, that's nice, sweetie," her mother replied, obviously distracted by something other than their conversation. Angeline heard the deep murmur of a man's voice in the background, followed by the sound of lips kissing. She could only imagine what her mother was up to.

"Mom, it sounds like you're busy."

"What?" Her mother clicked back into the conversation. "No, David just got home."

"David?" Angeline yawned. Another month, another man. Her mother had relationship ADHD.

"Yes, darling, I'm sure I told you about him," she laughed airily.

"I'm sure you did," Angeline replied, already bored with this line of conversation.

She wondered what it would be like to have a mother who was more mature than hers was. Her mother's life was spent pursuing flights of fancy. She espoused niceties that didn't mean anything. She offered advice that only a five-year-old would find useful. They had never been able to have a meaningful conversation because her mother never allowed herself to go more than cellophane deep. She wanted her mother to rise to the occasion, but she never did.

"You know what you need?" her mother giggled. "A break."

Angeline heard the male murmur in the background again.

"David thinks that since you are, you know, spiritual . . . Sedona would be exciting for you."

"Please don't discuss my problems with David," Angeline said, beginning to fume.

"Oh, honey, don't be so private. You're my daughter, and that means that from time to time you will come up in conversation."

"Just, Mom," Angeline stuttered. "Just . . ."

Suddenly, the line seemed dead.

"Mom?" She checked her phone and discovered that she had a full signal. "Figures." She threw her cell phone on the couch and ate another handful of popcorn.

Sedona.

Sedona.

Sedona.

The word resounded through her head repeatedly. She had never heard of Sedona before, yet the familiar sound of its name strummed her heartstrings. She was utterly resistant to the idea of following the advice of one of her mother's random boyfriends, yet she was also curious. She picked up her phone and typed the word *Sedona* into the Internet browser.

CHAPTER NINETEEN

"Now *this* is aromatherapy." Angeline breathed, stretching to sun her legs on the stone landing midway up Bell Rock. It felt completely natural for her to speak aloud to no one in particular. She was speaking to the wind, the sun, the red stone, the old juniper, every insect and bird that composed this perfect Sedona moment she found herself in. She spotted a bulbous black ant meandering on the rock beside her and picked it up. Its small legs tickled the back of her hand as she examined it.

"It turns out that David was right," she said to the ant. "Sedona *was* the perfect place for me to change my perspective. I wish that I could live here, just like you. Wouldn't that be nice?" She returned the ant to the ground and removed the white cowboy hat from the top of her head. She lay back to sun herself, placing the hat over her face for shade. The hat had belonged to her father and still carried the faint scent of his hair. It reminded her of simple summer days on the ranch, where she had plenty of breathing space and spent leisurely hours communing with the land.

"Excuse me, miss?" said a man with a southern twang.

"Yes?" She lifted her hat and squinted into the sun. A boy in his early twenties smiled earnestly. He possessed the sort of All-American appeal that belonged on a Wheaties box.

"Do you mind if I sit here with you?" he asked. "I wouldn't want to be a bother, but this is my favorite overlook."

"Of course," she allowed, shifting to the side.

"Are you enjoying Sedona?" he huffed as he crouched down to take his seat.

"Oh, yes. Very much," she said.

"Where you from?" he asked with casual interest.

"California. Los Angeles, actually."

"I remember my first time to the ocean. I'd never seen anything like it."

"This is pretty magnificent, too. I'd forgotten how much I love the isolation of nature. It's nothing like the city." She looked around appreciatively. "Do you live here?"

"Yes, ma'am. I moved here from Tennessee." He looked into the distance. "How long are you in town for?"

"Not much longer," Angeline confessed. "But I wish that I could stay."

"Why don't you?"

"I've run out of money."

"We have plenty of money here," he laughed. "You just gotta find it."

"Well, let me know if you find any."

"You'll be the first." He chuckled.

"I'm Angeline," she offered, shifting to face him. "What's your name?"

"Rooster."

"That's a funny name."

"I'm a morning person," he explained. A blush bloomed on his cheeks, and he looked down. He was too cute for words.

"Well, Rooster." Angeline brushed the red dust from her hat. "I am glad to meet you. I think that I'm gonna conclude my trip with a nice long hike before the sun sets."

"Good luck," he said. "If you find your way back into town, stop by for a visit. I work at the fueling station in Oak Creek."

"I will if I do," she promised.

Angeline broke a good sweat hiking around the base of Bell Rock. She found shelter from the sun under an old juniper tree, resting her head against the trunk. After what seemed like only moments, she opened her eyes and was surprised to discover that the sun had dipped past the horizon. She hastily gathered her belongings and tread the path to her car in order to avoid stumbling in the dark. Just as the night sky turned black and a zillion stars twinkled above her head, she reached her car.

"Whoa," she breathed, admiring the full moon over the top of Bell Rock. She turned over the key and the fuel gauge on her car tinged. "Oh, come on," she complained.

CHAPTER TWENTY

Please See Cashier, the electronic display flashed on the credit card reader at the pump. Angeline returned the card to her wallet and stepped out of the crisp windy night into the convenience store.

"Angeline!" Rooster's voice twanged with enthusiasm.

"Hi, Rooster."

"I wasn't expecting to see you so soon."

"I needed gas," she explained, handing her debit card over the counter.

"Did you find your pot of gold yet?" he asked hopefully.

"Not yet." She smiled. "This is my last stop."

"What you need is to catch a leprechaun."

"You're very helpful."

The entrance door dinged to indicate someone had entered the store.

"Is someone looking for a leprechaun?" a blonde woman with a thick Irish accent asked. Her sun-kissed skin was accented by glittering diamonds that were a bit flamboyant for this simple mountain town. Her clothes, all the colors of the rainbow, were well matched in style, if not hue. Yet, the mix and match was charming. She looked like a bag of Skittles held in a sparkling crystal dish.

"Look—you found one!" Rooster laughed.

"You certainly did. I'm Allison." She smiled, tossing her keys onto the counter. "And there is your leprechaun." She pointed to the keychain on the counter, which featured a Swarovski crystal leprechaun with a green hat and rosy cheeks, sitting on a rainbow.

The three looked at the leprechaun's face smiling up at them and laughed.

"Follow the rainbow . . ." Rooster warbled as he traced his finger across the ornament, "and find your pot of gold." His finger landed on the acrylic display that held dollar scratch lottery tickets. He looked up expectantly.

"All right—give me one of those," Angeline moaned in surrender. She reached into her wallet. "My last dollar," she confessed.

"Good luck." He tore the ticket off the roll and

handed it to her.

"Here goes nothing." She borrowed a penny from the penny jar and scratched the silver paint off of the ticket, "And . . . nothing," Angeline said quietly, scarcely disguising her disappointment.

"That won't do." Allison furrowed her brow. She reached into her purse and pulled out a handful of crisp one-dollar bills. "Let's try again. Six tickets please."

Rooster counted six tickets and handed them to Allison, who tore three from the row and handed them to Angeline.

"Oh, no." Angeline held her hand up in objection. "That's really nice of you, but not necessary."

"You asked to meet a leprechaun—and you did. You have to follow the magic to find the gold." Her eyes sparkled with amusement.

"Okay. I'll give it a shot." Angeline shrugged.

She scratched the first ticket.

"One hundred and fifty dollars!" she exclaimed.

"No way!" Rooster laughed in congratulations.

"Try the next one," Allison encouraged.

Angeline scratched the second ticket.

"Fifty dollars," she laughed. "I don't believe it." Her hand shook as she scratched the third ticket. Her head snapped up in disbelief. "Five thousand dollars."

"Are you kidding me?" Rooster's eyes widened twice their size as he examined the three consecutive winning tickets. He turned to Allison and pointed to the three unscratched tickets in her hand. "Can I have one of those?"

"Sure." She shrugged her shoulders easily and handed him a ticket.

The three leaned into a huddle and watched with rapt attention as the coin scratched the silver paint.

"Not a winner." He turned his attention to Allison. "Try the other ones."

A quick flick of the wrist revealed that they weren't winners either. Both Allison and Rooster looked to Angeline.

"Holy cow," Rooster breathed. "I wouldn't have believed it if I didn't see it for myself."

"Looks like your leprechaun really was lucky," Angeline laughed nervously.

"That wasn't just luck," Allison foretold. "Sedona has a plan for you."

"Let me split it with you," Angeline offered.

"No way," Allison objected. "I can't explain it, but that miracle was meant for you alone."

"Can I redeem these here?" Angeline asked as she turned to Rooster.

"We don't have that much cash on hand. You'll need to drive to Phoenix and redeem them at the State Lottery Office. It is a bit of a process," he explained.

Angeline furrowed her brow, calculating the remaining money in her checking account in order to ascertain how many days until her account ran dry. She was getting dangerously close to a zero balance. Allison noticed her contemplation and stepped forward.

"I have to go to Phoenix this week. Why don't I write you a check for the full amount?" she offered helpfully. "That way you can cash it today and just focus on why Sedona decided to keep you."

"Are you sure?" Angeline exhaled. "That would make things much easier."

"I would be delighted," Allison said enthusiastically.

"This is surreal," Angeline breathed, looking from side to side.

"This place is." Allison cast Rooster a conspiratorial glance and pulled a silver checkbook and pen from her purse, "Let's get you on your way. What is your name, dear?"

"Angeline Bridges." Angeline poked her head over Allison's shoulder and spelled her name as she filled the check out. Allison presented the check to her with an open palm, as if bestowing a gift upon royalty.

"Good luck," Allison said, with a half bow.

"Thank you." Angeline bowed back as they exchanged the money note for the scratch tickets.

Allison fanned herself with the tickets. "And now, I am off to the Arizona State lottery office with my *three* winning tickets!" Before she exited the store she paused, turning to offer one final piece of advice. "Hey, Angeline?"

"Yeah?" Angeline replied, still a bit dazed.

"Don't let this be your one Sedona story. There's a journey here for you. Just stay open."

"I will, Allison," Angeline promised.

"Good luck to you." Allison nodded her head and disappeared into the Sedona night.

Angeline looked at the check in her hands and whistled, "Good-bye *Super Eight*. Hello luxury."

"Upgrading your accommodations?" Rooster asked with a smirk.

"Definitely," Angeline agreed. "Do you have any suggestions?"

"BOS Retreat Center in Uptown."

"Does it have a spa?"

"I believe it does."

"I'm sold."

CHAPTER TWENTY-ONE

"There are meetings, and there are *meetings*." Toby cut into his filet and took a bite. His cufflink glimmered in the afternoon sun and refracted a spot of light that jumped across his lunch companion's face. For amusement, he intentionally held his wrist in that position, so as to reflect light into the gentleman's eye.

"The outcome of this meeting could make or break your company." Toby set his fork on his plate and touched the corner of his mouth with white linen. "Your company stock has tanked. You are on the down-slide. You know it, and I know it. I hold the key for you to recover not only your company, but multiply your assets tenfold within six months."

"What will it cost me?" asked Donnie Anderson, the owner of Donnie Oil, who sat across the table from him.

"You aren't asking the right question." Toby took a sip of his cocktail. "The question isn't what it will cost, but what you will gain. And the answer is a whole lot. The information I am about to give you will change the face of the energy industry and position you at the top of it."

"And the way that you acquired this information . . . is it legal?"

"Unorthodox, perhaps, but not illegal." Toby watched as the server set another drink on the table and collected their dishes. "It was gained in a sector that I would call the gray area."

"This gray area, is there any way that it could lead back to you?"

"Not in a million years," Toby smirked.

"And it's legal?" Donnie asked again.

"In a manner of speaking, yes."

"What *is* this information?" Donnie sat back in his chair.

"Do you think I'm running a charity?" Toby held his gaze. "You have to trade something."

"What?"

"A favor."

"What kind of favor?"

"The unspecified kind. The day will come when I

need you to do something, and you'll have to do it without hesitation or question."

"A blank check?" Donnie shifted uncomfortably. "Christ, Toby, are you in the Mafia now?"

"I'm offering to put you in a position of power that you've never fathomed before, one that will enable you to write a check that will cover a hundred times what you have access to now."

"And it requires a favor?" Donnie reaffirmed, contemplating.

"A *one-time* favor," Toby emphasized.

Toby watched multiple streams of dialogue flash across Donnie's forehead. Five out of the six conversations that ran through his mind were in favor of the trade, but that singular voice of conscience threatened to dissuade him. Toby had to make sure that didn't happen.

"You have twenty seconds before I get up and walk away from this table. I came to you first because I want to see you take the dominant seat in the industry, but there are twenty others with half your virtue and twice your guts who would trade their eyeteeth for this information."

The synapses lit in Donnie's brain like fireworks. Toby looked at his watch.

"Ten . . . nine . . . eight . . . seven . . . six . . ."

Toby stood up.

"Five . . . four . . . three . . . two . . ."

Toby turned and walked away from the table.

"Wait," Donnie called after him.

Toby turned around.

"I'm in," Donnie stated.

"Seven words: Merger. Donnie Oil. Chesapeake Energy. Hostile Takeover." Toby counted the words on his fingers. "As soon as I walk away from this table, call your attorneys and set it up. As of ten minutes ago, they're vulnerable."

"No," Donnie breathed, calculating the implications of buying out the largest energy company in the United States.

"You're welcome," Toby smiled as he walked away.

With seven words he'd created a powerful ally—a move that would someday prove to be pivotal.

CHAPTER TWENTY-TWO

"I'm bored with you people. I don't know why I bother having you over. If it wasn't so depressing, I'd just drink alone." Toby took a puff of his cigar and blew a smoke ring. The twenty-some guests around the table in his executive apartment laughed. But he wasn't joking.

"At least one of you brought someone interesting." His eyes locked with a blonde woman's striking green eyes. She had introduced herself as Sarah. "Join me on the balcony?" he asked.

"The balcony?" Her eyes shifted around the table uncomfortably.

Toby stood and extended his palm. "To look at the stars."

"You can't see the stars in Manhattan."

"I have a telescope."

"I'm here with someone," she protested.

"Not anymore." He turned to her date. "Get out," he ordered without a flinch.

"Excuse me?" Her date was momentarily stunned by Toby's rudeness.

"Frank, he's drunk," Sarah's voice dropped in a smooth warning.

"You heard me," Toby slurred. "You are dismissed."

"Sarah, let's get out of here," Frank commanded heroically as he abruptly stood. He turned to face Toby and puffed out his chest, which was formidable in size. Multiple chairs scraped across the floor with a screech as the men around the table shot to their feet to intervene. Toby laughed, standing to meet the challenge. He rocked slightly on unstable feet.

He turned to Sarah. "That's quite a fancy rough-and-tumble hulk that you've got there. Does he turn green, too?" His laugh was cut short by a thud, followed by an explosion of pain in his left eye. He toppled backward as Frank leapt forward in attack. Multiple layers of commotion overlapped at once: glass breaking, dishes falling to the floor, horrified feminine shrieks, the multi-toned hollering of men. It took the varied efforts of three men to pull Frank away from Toby, who had fallen into a crumpled heap on the floor.

"Get him out of here!" Toby yelled, wiping blood from the corner of his mouth.

"You have a mob to do your dirty work?" Frank yelled as they ejected him from the apartment. "Come out here and face me like a man, you dirty drunk!"

The three men closed the door and locked it to keep Frank from initiating a second round of brute force. He pounded on the door and hollered for Sarah to come out. Kelly, the brunette at the table, rushed to Toby's aid. She held her cloth napkin to his bleeding brow.

Sarah looked at Toby. He read her mind clearly. She was disgusted.

"I think you'd better go," he said quietly.

She grabbed her handbag and walked out. The defiant click of her heels on the wood floor echoed through the apartment, and the door was opened to provide her safe passage to the hallway.

Instead of seeing the faces of his eighteen remaining dinner guests when he looked around the room, he saw his most frequent nightmare flash before his eyes. His grandmother's damning gaze, his father's angry bellow, every person who hated him for manipulating them or using them for his gain. The angry mob of faces twisted with rage and yelled accusations as they closed in upon him until his heels were backed against the edge of a cliff, leaving him only two options—face his demons or jump.

He always jumped.

"I need a drink, Kelly," he said to the brunette, pushing himself to his feet.

"What kind of drink?" she asked. Kelly was a recent addition to the same Manhattan social circle that Toby ran with. She was the daughter of some important congressman.

"A strong one," he replied.

"I'll be right back," she promised, touching his face with concern.

He walked to the living room.

"Toby." Charlie, one of his work associates, put his hand on Toby's shoulder.

"Not now, Charlie." Toby pushed him off and morosely sank into the brown leather chair.

Charlie sighed in resignation and joined the remaining guests as they politely tended to the broken glass and various dishes of fine food cast onto the floor. When Kelly returned, Toby took the glass and drank it in one long gulp.

"Better?" she asked.

"Not hardly," he said.

"Why do you do that?"

"Do what?"

"Make trouble for yourself," she said, her forehead revealing just how grossly he had humiliated himself. He took a deep breath to clear his misery.

"I'm not sure," he confessed. "Have you ever had a gun held to your head?"

"No," she replied.

"I have." He tipped his glass to take the last drop of whiskey in his mouth. "I've made a lot of good people mad at me."

Suddenly, the air pressure in the room shifted. The room warmed and smelled like flowers. A tender and celestial female voice echoed around him.

It's not your fault.

"What?" he asked.

"I didn't say anything," Kelly replied.

The maternal voice repeated, *It's not your fault.*

Toby looked around the room wildly, seeking the source of this phantom voice.

All of the things that you have done were part of a destined process. You are a great man. More than anyone, you are a rare and precious gem.

He covered his ears to block out the voice. It didn't work.

It is time to remember your true identity.

Pressing the spot between his brows, he concentrated to hear the voice more distinctly.

Sedona.

"Sedona?" he asked aloud.

"No—Kelly." Kelly touched his temple, "Are you okay? You might have hit your head."

Toby felt something hot pressing against his chest. He stuck his hand in his suit jacket and pulled out the thimble-sized bronze mirror that his grandmother had given him. It shone like a night-light.

"Pretty," Kelly breathed. She reached to touch it. "What is it?"

"Nothing." He closed his palm quickly. "I have to go."

"Where?" She was startled.

"Sedona," he replied.

"Why?"

"Because the voice told me to."

"You're kind of troubled, aren't you?"

"You have no idea," he confessed.

"I think you should lie down; you're pretty drunk."

"Darling," he slurred, looking at his closed palm, from which the light from the bronze mirror peeked through his fingers. "I've experienced things that you could never fathom. I have to go to Sedona, now."

"Why?" She was confused.

"To find out."

"What?"

"Exactly." He touched her cheek and rose from his chair. Before he knew it, he was walking the city streets. His face bore the bruises of the recent conflict but his heart bore the much deeper wounds of his life of unchecked excess. He felt like he was being strangled. He didn't have space to think. He could hardly breathe. He had to get out of town.

He hailed a cab.

"Where to?" The cab driver set the meter.

"JFK," Toby answered, using his handkerchief to scrub the blood from his face.

CHAPTER TWENTY-THREE

Noah felt like a kite drifting in the sky without a string. Since meeting Mago on Bell Rock three years ago, he had returned every morning at daybreak and found her waiting for him. They shared insights and recounted stories as mother and son became reacquainted upon the bedrock of their mutual hope for humanity.

Using Mago's vision for humanity as inspiration, Noah had built the BOS Resort and Healing Center in an effort to transform her dream into reality. This quest provided him endless inspiration and a mighty sense of purpose. After all the years of cutting independence, it turned out that he was a mama's boy after all. He did Mother Earth's bidding without question and loved every minute of it.

His well-being was turned on end when he returned

to Bell Rock a week ago, and she hadn't been there to greet him. He waited for hours and encountered nothing but the morning silence. The following six days she hadn't come either. Her sudden departure filled Noah with an enormous sense of loss.

To make matters worse, everything at the BOS Resort, where he managed day-to-day operations, reminded him of her. Every morning when he drove in and saw the sculpture at the entrance depicting the two hemispheres of the brain with LED lights that wove through its folds firing like synapses, his heart dropped. She'd been particularly inspired by this sculpture because it symbolized the philosophy by which she had created this resort and healing center, the Brain Operating System.

The ChunBuKyung inlaid in the lobby ceiling, carved from onyx, and the golden characters that spelled *Chun-Hwa* above the lecture hall—the Korean phrase meaning the completion of the human soul—were also her design. Mago's spirit had built every square inch of this resort, and her unexplained departure left Noah feeling empty inside. He couldn't fathom where she had gone and why she wouldn't have told him that she was leaving. He felt utterly abandoned.

Noah's attention was drawn to the reception desk by

the sound of arguing. A woman with gold-spun curls emphatically waved her arms as she spoke. "I know that this isn't your fault. I know that, but I am asking for your help."

"Ms. Bridges, your card has been declined," answered Holly, the front desk attendant with mousy brown hair and kind eyes.

"I know that. What I am trying to tell you is that I don't have any other way to pay right now."

"Without payment, you will have to vacate your room." Holly was apologetic. "I'm sorry, but those are the rules."

"Listen, I'm not trying to pull anything. I just need time to figure out what happened with my bank account."

"We take credit cards," Holly offered.

"I told you, I don't have enough on my credit card."

"Is there someone who can help you?"

"How about this—what if I give you the keys to my car?"

"I'm sorry but I can't take a car as payment."

"Not as payment. Just as a deposit while I figure out the payment."

Noah strode to the reception desk to help his employee resolve the dispute.

"Excuse me, miss?" He touched the blonde woman's

shoulder. "Can I help you?"

When she turned around, Noah felt as if the breath was knocked out of him. He couldn't believe what he saw. *Mother Mago.*

"You're here," he breathed.

"Yes," she answered.

"How?"

"Excuse me?"

Noah looked at her for a long time. It wasn't Mago. But their faces looked just alike, literally every feature, down to the aqua eyes. However, there were two notable differences: this woman had physical form and blonde curls. "You look just like . . ." He tried to find a way to explain.

"I know." She smiled, holding her hand up in a pose. "The Mentos commercial, right?"

"No." Noah was confused.

"*DeLeu Towers*?" she guessed.

"No."

"Performances in the Park?"

"No," he laughed. "I was going to say that you are the spitting image of my mother."

Holly and the blonde woman looked at each other doubtfully. Noah was a black man with dark skin, and she was a white woman with golden curls.

She raised an eyebrow. "Were you adopted?"

Noah realized the absurdity of his claim. "Something like that." He changed the subject. "Is there a problem here?"

"Yes," she breathed, ready to dive into an explanation. "I have been staying here for the past two days. I came down today to extend my reservation, and my debit card was declined. I still have a room deposit with you, and I wanted to use that credit as payment for another night while I figure out what is going on with my bank account but—"

"I see," Noah interrupted. "I think we can work something out."

She exhaled in relief. "Thank you."

"You're welcome." He turned to Holly. "Please make sure that Ms. . . ."

"Bridges," the blonde said. "Angeline Bridges."

"Right." Noah cleared his throat. "That Ms. Bridges has accommodations for as long as she needs."

"Of course, Dr. Whitley." Holly nodded her head. "Well then, Ms. Bridges, we are all set."

"Do I need to sign anything?" Angeline asked.

"No. Have a nice stay." Holly smiled.

Angeline turned to Noah. "Thank you. I will repay you as soon as I can."

"I'm sure you will, Ms. Bridges." He smiled. "You are our most welcome guest."

"Is this because I look like your mother?"

"Perhaps," he admitted. "It does evoke a certain protectiveness."

"Be sure to thank your mother for me."

"I most certainly will," he promised, leading her through the lobby. "Are you planning on staying in Sedona long?"

"As long as I can."

"Have you found employment yet?"

"I haven't settled long enough to look."

"We are looking for a back office assistant. Would you be interested in interviewing?" Of course, the job was already hers, but Noah decided to take her through an interview process in the name of routine.

"I would." Angeline beamed. "I love it here."

"Let's meet in the lobby at three. I have someone I want you to meet." He was anxious to get Suna's opinion. This woman really was the spitting image of Mago, and she had appeared in his hotel lobby after Mago's spirit had unexplainably disappeared from Bell Rock.

It was a most perplexing turn of events.

CHAPTER TWENTY-FOUR

"When will Suna be available?"

Suna's assistant tapped the screen of his tablet. "She has back-to-back sessions all day."

"That won't do. Thank you, anyway." Noah opened the door to the auditorium. Suna stood on the stage, leading the crowded room through a vibrational training. Noah remembered his first time in one of these high-spirited sessions. It had taken him a while to become comfortable finding and following his own rhythm. His inclination when he moved his body to music was to perform a fancy jig to impress a crowd— like an eighteen-year-old on an episode of *Soul Train*— versus focusing inside and tapping into his internal rhythm. When he was finally able to overcome his need for recognition, his efforts paid off.

Even though the lights were dimmed, he was certain she would feel his presence. She was quite sensitive, able to detect the subtle shift of an insect's wings. As expected, her eyes opened, and she met his gaze. He motioned toward the door. She nodded.

Noah looked at his watch and walked with purpose to the lobby where Angeline was waiting. She wore an aquamarine boatneck T-shirt and a freshly ironed pair of white linen pants. Her tanned ankles were accented by crisp white Keds.

"You look like a breath of fresh air," Noah greeted her. "That color looks very nice on you."

"It's my lucky color."

"Lucky color?" Noah raised an eyebrow.

"Every time I wear it, things seem to go smoothly. And I really want this job," she confided.

"If I found a color that looked as nice on me, I would consider myself lucky, as well. It matches the color of your eyes, exactly." He shook his head. "So strange."

"What's strange?"

"You really are the spitting image of Mago."

"Your mother?"

"My mother," he confirmed. "Aquamarine is significant to her, as well."

"Huh," she laughed nervously. "Aren't we supposed

to be meeting someone?" She looked around the lobby.

"Indeed," he confirmed. "She will be along soon. In the meantime, why don't I show you around?"

They walked the estate. Noah found that as he showed Angeline every detail of the property, he felt as if he were giving the grand tour to Mago herself. It was both comforting and confusing to be in her presence.

"And our tour concludes here." Noah opened a plate-glass door to a fish-bowl office completely encased by windows. The Sedona wilderness was displayed on one side of the desk and the lobby of the resort on the other.

"Whoa," Angeline breathed. "This is spectacular." She walked around the office, touching all of the glass surfaces. "It looks like a crystal palace."

Noah's heart took a double beat. The *Crystal Palace* was the name of the sanctuary beneath Bell Rock where he had first met Mago. "What did you say?" He tried to control the tempo of his voice.

"I was just saying how beautiful this office is." She turned toward him.

"I'm glad that you like it. This will be your station of command."

"Mine?" she breathed.

"Yes," he confirmed with a nod.

Angeline looked around the room, awed by this

revelation. "What position am I interviewing for again?"

"Initially, I wanted to hire you as an office assistant, but now that we have spent time together, I think that we can use you in a number of ways."

"Like how?" She cocked her head.

"Before I get ahead of myself, please sit down." He motioned to the chair behind the desk. She sat down and placed her hands on the glass tabletop in front of her.

"How does it feel?" Noah asked.

"Amazing."

"Take it for a spin."

"What?"

"Take it for a spin." He whirled his finger around. "You won't know if it's truly yours until you have spun in it."

"This is the strangest job interview I have ever been on."

"This won't be like any job you have ever had," he promised. "Spin."

"If you insist." She spun around in the chair with the zest of Wonder Woman. Her golden curls bounced.

"Well?" he asked.

"It's mine," she affirmed.

"I'm glad." Noah sat in the chair opposite the glass top desk. "How did you end up here?"

"In Sedona?"

"At the BOS Resort."

"It was recommended to me by an employee of a local gas station." Angeline recounted the story of meeting Rooster during her final hike on Bell Rock, which then led to Allison and her lucky leprechaun, the three winning lottery tickets, and the personal check exchanged for the winning tickets—which had bounced.

"And those events led to you to the argument with my employee in reception?"

"It was a weird moment," she explained. "I was distressed because my checking account had overdrafted. I mean, what kind of person buys you lottery tickets, acts like they are overjoyed when you win, and then steals your tickets under the guise of making your life more convenient?" Angeline blustered.

"It seems to me like she did you a favor." Noah leaned back in his chair.

"Excuse me?" Angeline was beside herself.

"This woman helped you break down the limiting information in your brain."

"I think what she really broke was my spirit." Angeline's voice dropped.

"Think about it. Had that situation unfolded any differently than it did, you would have gone back to Los Angeles. I never would have seen you making a ruckus in the lobby, we never would have met, and you wouldn't have this job. Your inclination was to return home when you ran out of money. . . . Of all the possible outcomes, following that instinct would have limited your options down to *one*. Because she gave you the temporary illusion of resources, your options multiplied exponentially and put you into a situation that you would have never otherwise experienced."

"Wow," she said. "You aren't afraid of the fancy words, are you?"

He laughed.

"I betcha you have a big fancy degree, don't cha?" she laughed.

"I have a few," he admitted.

"It shows." She sparkled.

Their conversation was interrupted when Suna entered the room. "Hello, I—" Suna's easy smile was wiped from her lips when she saw Angeline's face. Noah quickly stood.

"Suna, I'd like you to meet Angeline," he interjected before Suna could say a word.

"Hi, I'm Angeline." Angeline offered her hand. "It's nice to meet you."

"The pleasure is mine." Suna recovered quickly. She shook Angeline's hand and cast a questioning glance at

Noah. Of course, he knew exactly what she was thinking. The same thing that he had thought. *Mother Mago.*

"Suna, please have a seat. We were just discussing a possible job opportunity here for Angeline. She's new to Sedona and looking for employment."

"All right." Suna sat. "Tell me a little about yourself."

"Well, I was an actress in California. I am twenty-six years old. I used to have a cat. And I've never really had a regular job. I have pretty much modeled and acted for the past eight years."

"Previous office experience is valued, but there is a greater value we seek from our employees at the BOS Resort. We have a mission—do you know what it is?" Suna asked.

"Relaxation?" Angeline answered uncertainly.

"We offer programs that bring people back to a more natural state of being. We believe that when the world is filled with such people, it will naturally breed more peaceful situations. We cultivate a nurturing environment for both our staff and our guests." Suna leaned forward.

"That's awesome." Angeline's eyes sparkled.

"What do you think is the best solution for the plight of humanity?" Suna asked, attempting to gauge Angeline's level of awareness.

"To be honest, I haven't thought about it." Angeline looked down. "I guess have been too preoccupied with my own problems."

"That's natural," Suna assured her.

"It is?" Angeline looked up.

"The natural trajectory for the growth of a soul is to first sort out our own problems and get to know our true selves. Once those issues have been worked out, it creates space in the mind to focus on the health of our community. After that, your awareness will grow to encompass the whole world."

Angeline didn't seem to know how to respond. It was obviously a wider vantage point than she had ever contemplated.

"You know what she would be perfect for?" Suna clapped, as if something had just occurred to her. She turned to Noah.

"What's that?" Noah asked with a smirk.

"The Vortex Tours." Suna beamed.

"The Vortex Tours?" Angeline asked.

"Yes," Suna breathed. "I'll train you how to feel the energy from the vortexes in Sedona, and you can take others out and teach them how to feel the energy and meditate. Would you like that?"

"Oh yes, very much," Angeline agreed.

Noah interjected, "And you can work with me in the office the rest of your time. We can split your time fifty/fifty. How does that sound?"

"Like my dream job," Angeline sighed wistfully.

The three laughed. Angeline blushed.

"Well, I think that concludes our interview." Noah rose from his seat. "When do you think that you can you start?"

"Tomorrow."

"Perfect. Meet me in your office at eight." Noah shook her hand.

"It was nice to meet you," Suna offered.

"I'm excited to work with both of you." Angeline was positively alight with inspiration.

"As are we." Noah placed his hand on her shoulder as they escorted her out of the office.

They watched her golden curls bounce as she bopped through the lobby toward the guest rooms.

"What do you think?" Noah asked.

"I think it has begun," Suna stated.

"My heart began to beat irregularly when I met her," he confided.

"It will pass," she assured him. "It won't be long until the other two come."

"Do you think she knows?" Noah asked her as he

motioned toward Angeline in the lobby.

"No." She shook her head. "I don't think that she has any idea. We must do everything that we can to support her until she remembers."

"Of all the luck . . ." Noah whistled.

"It wasn't luck, Hwanggung. It was destiny."

CHAPTER TWENTY-FIVE

The symphony that filled the cabin of the plane filtered into Toby's ears like nails on a chalkboard. Hundreds of metallic clicks, a murmur of voices, throats clearing, people coughing, a baby crying. He hated flying commercial. At least he was in first class, where his tall frame wouldn't have to fold upon itself like a lawn chair in storage. He resolved to get a strong drink and doze.

When Toby raised his head in pursuit of the flight attendant, he noticed a burly Hispanic man with a pronounced limp enter the plane, an army-green canvas satchel hoisted over his shoulder. He was handsome and huge. A bear of a man. He had to be at least six-foot-five with a gentle yet commanding presence. Toby couldn't tear his eyes away from his forehead, which bore a singular unchanging symbol rather than the typical stream of dialogue that flowed across the forehead of every other person he had encountered since receiving the bronze mirror. The center point of this man's brow was branded with a sword of white light that shone out in gentle rays, illuminating his face.

He sat next to Toby. He smelled like the desert and filled up the entire seat and a good two inches of Toby's, as well.

"I'm Leuters." His voice, gruff and deep in octave, was seasoned with a thick Spanish accent that was difficult to understand.

"Toby," he answered, still staring.

"Phoenix?" Leuters asked.

"Phoenix–Sedona," Toby responded.

"Same," Leuters huffed. "Renting car?"

"Yes," Toby answered, still in awe.

"We share," Leuters said, not as a question but rather as a fact.

"Sure." Toby found Leuters's direct nature refreshing.

Leuters closed his eyes and went immediately to sleep, leaving Toby with his thoughts. Toby instantly liked this man. Even the deep melodic sound of his snore was comforting, like a cat's soft purr.

***

"Where are you from?" Toby asked, accelerating the car and setting the cruise control.

"Mexico," Leuters replied. He did not ask where Toby was from.

"What brings you to Sedona?" Toby asked, content to carry the conversation.

"Red rocks." Leuters looked out the window. "And you?"

"A mysterious voice," Toby replied simply.

"Humph." Leuters chuckled and tapped his chest once. "I had a dream."

"Really?" Toby asked. "How did you end up in New York?"

"I dream I saw sword on red rock." He opened his satchel and pulled out a postcard and handed it to Toby. "I go to Timna Valley. Next dream showed Bell Rock. Came back."

"Where's Timna Valley?" Toby asked.

"Israel." Leuters chortled.

"That's a long detour," Toby whistled. "Would've been helpful to have dreamed of Bell Rock in the first place."

"Wouldn't meet you." Leuters took the postcard back and stuffed it into his canvas bag.

Toby considered his answer. "Interesting way of looking at it."

"Humans move around planet. Flow lead to destiny."

"Do you think our meeting is destiny?"

"We together now. Destiny," Leuters answered affirmatively.

Toby burned with curiosity because of the sword branded on his companion's forehead. He wanted to inquire about the unreadable difference of Leuters's system of thought, but he had never revealed his gift before for fear of losing the upper hand.

"No upper hand," Leuters answered his thought. "Ask."

Toby almost died from shock. The car swerved off the road. He fought to recover control by pulling the steering wheel hard to the left, which returned the tires safely to the road. "Excuse me?"

"Ask question," Leuters commanded.

"I don't have a question," Toby lied.

"Very well," Leuters conceded, content to look out the window.

They drove in silence for a full hour. Meanwhile, Toby's thoughts went crazily in every direction. His one question multiplied into a hundred, and he was paranoid that Leuters was reading every single one of them.

"You need drink?" Leuters broke the silence.

"What?" Toby's paranoia went into overdrive.

"Your hand." Leuters pointed at Toby's trembling hand on the steering wheel.

"I have a condition," Toby lied as he shook his hand out.

Leuters laughed. "Drinking fix condition?" His eyes sparkled.

"That's private." Toby was offended.

"Nothing private," Leuters said. "Ask."

Toby decided to finally ask the question that had haunted him the past hour: "Can you read my mind?"

"I hear in head."

"Hmmm." Toby considered. "That must be annoying." He couldn't imagine having everyone else's voices intruding like that. It was hard enough to read another's thoughts, but at least he could look away or put down the bronzed trinket.

"Like solitude," Leuters admitted. Before Toby could reveal his greatest secret to this complete stranger, Leuters answered his thought. "I know," he said simply.

"Yeah," Toby concurred. "I figured."

Again they drove in silence, both listening to the whir of the tires and watching the gradual transformation of desert landscapes from yellow to red.

CHAPTER TWENTY-SIX

"It's just a hop, skip and a jump away from here," Angeline sang enthusiastically. "And right around this boulder . . ." She held the hand of Mabel, a guest on her Vortex Tour.

"Oh my dear, sweet goodness," Mabel breathed when she saw the 360-degree view of Sedona from the top of Airport Mesa.

"Oh my dear, sweet goodness," Angeline agreed. "Would you like to meditate now? I can teach you how to feel the energy rising from the Earth. You can really feel it here because the wattage is higher. It's remarkable." Angeline widened her eyes for emphasis. She took a seat on the ground and brushed a few pebbles from the spot beside her. Mabel positioned her rotund backside over the spot and slowly lowered her seventy-year-old frame to the ground.

"I'm a comin' . . ." she snickered.

"I'm a waitin' . . ." Angeline laughed.

Angeline led her through a simple meditation that caused tears to spring to Mabel's eyes. She moved her prescription glasses to the side and wiped the moisture from her cheeks.

"You're really good at that. I can really feel the sweetness of your heart." Mabel laughed at herself for crying so easily. "Oh, I do love it here," she sighed. "I've been here thirteen times, and I never get tired of it."

"You should move here," Angeline suggested.

Mabel laughed. "Oh, darlin' . . . I've got me a man at home that don't get out of his *Lazy Boy* long enough to get his'self an ice tea, much less pack up a whole house worth of stuff and move to this one-horse mountain town." She patted the back of Angeline's hand. "But I'm sure glad that you moved here. You promise me that you will always follow your dreams."

"I promise." Angeline's heart went out to this old woman. She seemed to be struggling from a lack of inspiration in her life.

"No man is better than the wrong man." Mabel looked wistfully into the distance. "I sure wish someone woulda told me that when I was your age. But enough about me and my troubles. Tell me, how long have you been here?"

"Three months," Angeline answered.

"Is that all?" Mabel breathed. "You seem like you have been here for ages, leading me up that hill like you were some sorta billy goat, or something." She patted her hand again. "You done real good for yourself."

"I'm finally happy," Angeline confided, just above a whisper.

"I sure am glad," Mabel answered. "Ain't nothin' more important than that."

After a lovely afternoon touring Sedona, Mabel and Angeline returned to the resort. Mabel stood at the reception desk and waved goodbye to Angeline. She leaned in and whispered to the front desk agent, "I don't know where you got her, but she is a real gem."

Angeline smiled to herself. She felt like every person who walked through the doors of the BOS Resort was her family. She examined her clipboard, turned around, and tried to identify her next VIP tour guest.

"Toby?" she called through the lobby.

"Angeline?" She heard the surprised voice of a woman.

She looked about the room and saw the woman with the lucky leprechaun who wore all the colors of the rainbow and spoke with a thick Irish accent.

"Allison? What are you doing here?"

"I am a member here." Allison jumped into Angeline's embrace. "What are you doing here?"

"I work here." She held out her clipboard as if brandishing the sword from the stone.

"Of all the places in all the world . . ." Allison sang.

"No kidding." Angeline touched her arm. "I've been hoping that I would run into you."

"Really?"

"I wanted to thank you for what you did for me."

"Everything worked out?"

"It did." Angeline paused. "There was some confusion with the bank, but after a few days the check that you wrote me cleared."

Allison's brow furrowed. "I'm sorry. I hope that it didn't cause you any stress."

"Actually," Angeline laughed. "It is how I found this job. So it all kind of worked out for the best."

"I'm delighted," Allison said.

"What are you doing here?"

"I'm here to see Suna. She commissioned me to complete a few paintings."

"You're an artist?" Angeline asked, though she could have guessed that just by looking at her.

"Guilty," Allison laughed airily. "We've been working

on a top secret project."

"Top secret?" Angeline raised an eyebrow.

"She has been closely guiding me through a series of paintings depicting Mother Earth." She paused. "You know, you look a lot like her."

"Like Suna?" Angeline would have been delighted to be compared to such a woman. Her gentle nature and authenticity set her apart from anyone Angeline had ever met.

"Like Mother Earth," Allison corrected. "She has copper skin and dark hair, but . . . your eyes."

Angeline chuckled and shrugged her shoulders. "You wouldn't believe how often I've heard that I look like somebody's moth—"

A drop dead gorgeous man in his thirties wearing a perfectly tailored business suit interrupted their conversation, "Excuse me, Miss?" he asked. "I was told that you were looking for me?"

She looked at her clipboard. "Toby?"

"That's me." He smiled.

Angeline looked him from head to toe. His expensive suit wasn't well matched for an afternoon outdoors. "You're scheduled for a Vortex Tour?"

"Indeed, I am," he confirmed.

Angeline turned to Allison and smiled apologetically.

"We'll have to catch up later."

"Of course." Allison nodded. "Talk soon. Have fun."

Angeline cleared her throat, addressing Toby, "Sorry about that. Small town."

"No problem," he said.

"Would you like to change your clothes?" she asked.

Toby looked down at his suit, "These are the only kind of clothes I have."

"I don't want you to ruin your suit."

"Really, it's no problem."

"If you're certain . . ."

"I am," he assured her.

"All right. Prepare yourself for the time of your life." Her curls bobbed as she walked. When she looked back, she noticed Toby admiring her long tan legs. Having obviously been caught, he shrugged his shoulders and laughed.

Angeline knew she should have been offended by this overt admiration of her body, but she wasn't. Something about the easy way that he reacted to being caught disarmed her.

She opened the front lobby door. "You first," she laughed, shaking her head. "You obviously can't be trusted to keep your eyes to yourself."

CHAPTER TWENTY-SEVEN

"I was under the impression that this would be a private tour," Toby grumbled to the person sitting next to him in the large passenger van. He had envisioned an afternoon alone with the leggy blonde with kind aqua eyes. He had been sorely mistaken.

"It's private," the gentleman responded. "It's exclusively for members and guests of BOS."

"What is BOS, anyway?" Toby asked, disgruntled. He wasn't pleased that he was forced to endure an entire afternoon with a gaggle of tourists, each wanting to know who he was and where he was from.

"Brain Operating System?" the man replied. "It's a philosophy that compares your brain to a computer CPU and likens your thoughts to the software that it runs as a way to create more control over how you experience your life. For instance, if you didn't want to feel so irritated right now, you could choose to turn off the bad-tempered program and run the grateful program."

Toby cast him a sidewise glance. "Thanks for the tip."

"Anytime," the gentleman chuckled.

"What's the story with that girl?" Toby motioned toward Angeline, who sat at the front of the bus.

"Her?" This time it was the man who gave Toby a sideways glance. "She's out of your league."

"How so?" Toby asked, amused by this man's assessment of his value. His life had taught him that he could have any woman he wanted, anytime, and he was certain that she was no exception.

"She has a sparkle," the man answered.

Toby looked at the man's name tag stuck to his chest. "Are you saying that I don't sparkle, Bob?"

"A woman like that only comes around once in a lifetime. I've been here fifty-four years and I've only seen one so far—*her*." He pointed to the front of the bus like an enamored schoolboy.

"Are you in line for a date?" Toby repressed a smirk.

The old man chuckled. "I'm in the long line of admirers, just like you."

"Well then, if you don't mind," said Toby, looking at

Angeline again, "I think I'm going to take a shot."

"I sure would like to see that," Bob laughed.

"You'll have a front row seat." Toby stood and made his way to the row behind Angeline. He leaned forward and spoke in her ear, "Where are you taking us?"

She looked up and smiled. "Bell Rock. Have you heard of it?"

"I've been there." It was where he had dropped Leuters off on his first day in Sedona.

"Oh good," she said. "I could use your help."

"I'm all yours." Toby watched her forehead as she comprehended his double meaning, caught off guard by his sensual undertone. "I'm happy to help," he amended.

Her thoughts calmed, and her face relaxed into a smile. She was glad that she had misinterpreted his advance. "How long are you in town for?" she asked easily.

"I'm not sure," he admitted.

"Are you here on vacation?"

"I'm here to figure some stuff out."

Angeline exhaled. "I know the feeling. You picked the best possible place for reinvention."

"Did you reinvent yourself here?"

"I found myself here." She blushed. "Who I was before was the invention."

Toby wanted to know more. "What was your most

important discovery so far?"

Angeline considered for a long while. "I guess that I just want to be happy."

"What makes you happy?" He raised an eyebrow.

"Making other people happy," she said.

Toby noticed that her left cuspid poked subtly over her lower lip when she smiled, a charming imperfection. "That's a tall order. Most people don't know what makes them happy."

"People are happiest when they are discovering new parts of themselves. Because of my work, I get to be a part of that process every single day. That makes me happy."

Her simple and sincere answer impressed him.

"Do you think that I know myself?" Toby asked.

"I think that if you did, you wouldn't be here."

"Do you think that I'm happy?"

Angeline blushed and looked down. He had put her on the spot. "I think that you've had a rough life, but you try to hide it," she answered quietly.

"What makes you think that?" He wasn't sure why but what she thought about him mattered.

"When I look at you, I see your face, but I can't see your spirit." She quickly added, "My spirit didn't shine through when I first got here, either. I was kind of dead inside. This place can breathe the life back into you, if you let it. We are each going through a process, even me."

He wasn't sure how to respond to that. He checked her forehead for more details. Her thoughts were gentle, focused solely on his well-being. "Do you have any brothers and sisters?" he asked, changing the subject.

"I'm an only child."

"Me, too."

When their eyes met, Toby understood for the first time the meaning behind the saying *the eyes are the windows of the soul*. Her windows were clear, and her soul looked out into the world without filter or judgment.

"Would you like to have a cup of coffee with me after the tour?" he asked softly.

Angeline blushed. Her forehead said *yes*. "I would like that."

The bus pulled into the north parking lot of Bell Rock. Angeline stood up and checked her clipboard, calling out to the crowd, "All right, everyone, we will start with a hike and then we'll have thirty minutes of free time. Please make sure that you have your sunscreen and water." She smiled at Toby. Dropping her voice to a whisper, she said, "Would you like to walk at the front near me? I will be giving a guided energy meditation."

"I wouldn't miss it for the world." He meant every word. There was something incredibly inviting about her. He hadn't trusted anyone since the death of his grandmother, but he sensed that Angeline was uniquely genuine. Bob was right: a woman like this only comes around once in a lifetime.

He was going to make sure that he was first in line.

***

"Would you like to take a walk?" Toby asked Angeline the moment that free time began.

She looked around at the group, uncertain if she should comply. She wanted to spend time with him, but she also thought it best to keep herself available in case any of the guests had a question. Toby read her mind.

"I did buy the VIP package," he flirted openly. "We won't go far."

Angeline bit the corner of her lip and nodded her head. He loved her smile. They walked in a comfortable silence, each hyperaware of the other. The heat in Angeline's body rose a degree, and it wasn't because of the afternoon sun.

"What do you want for your life?" she asked, walking slowly.

"I guess the same as anyone. To find the right girl,

buy a house, retire early, settle down."

"Let me guess, you're a lawyer, right?"

"Stockbroker."

"And you probably went to some fancy college?"

"Harvard."

"And you probably have loads of money."

"Buckets and buckets of it."

"But none of that made you happy," she guessed.

"Define happiness." His stride slowed.

"Happiness is falling asleep each night completely satisfied with the day, excited that you get to wake up in the morning and do it all again." There was a wistfulness about her. It wasn't the flaky kind, either. She was chock-full of inspiration.

"Do you feel that way?" He raised an eyebrow.

"These days, I do." She raised her face to the sun.

"And you don't want more for your life than this small town can offer?"

"This small town has everything I need. A job I adore, a continuous flow of new friends, time to myself, and just look around—it's a modern-day Eden."

"What about buckets and buckets of money?" he laughed.

"That would be nice, too."

"I'm sure that it is on its way. If I were money, I

could think of no one that I would rather be with than you," he said.

"That's a sweet thing to say," she giggled. "Let's hope you're right."

Their conversation was interrupted by the sound of rocks falling, the pained howl of a man, followed by multiple shrieks. Angeline's head snapped in the direction of the scream. One of her charges had slid down the side of the mountain, at least ten feet, to the landing below.

"Bob!" she yelled, running down the mountain. Toby was fast on her heels. Bob lay in a heap, his leg twisted unnaturally. "What happened?" she yelled, unable to control the volume of her voice.

"My leg . . ." he moaned.

Toby touched Bob's hip. "I think his hip is broken."

"Someone call 911!" Angeline called to the guests on the landing above. "Toby, support his leg," she ordered.

Toby touched Bob's leg and the older man screamed. "Angeline, I think it is much worse than we thought. His leg might be broken too."

"Bob, just breathe deeply," she coached him. Her body began to burn hot. She knew what was going to happen within moments. "Toby, go down to the parking lot and wave the ambulance in," she ordered, trying to get him to leave quickly.

"No way," he protested. "I'm not leaving you alone."

"Toby, leave!" she yelled, but it was too late. She felt the heat rise from her body into the space around her, encapsulating both Toby and Bob. The process of healing had begun. Without being manipulated, Bob's leg began to vibrate, slowly moving to its natural position. Startled, Toby let go and raised his hands into the air.

"What in the . . . ." He couldn't believe his eyes. Bob's leg was anchored back into its joint, his bones fused back together. "Holy shit!" He met her gaze.

"Please don't tell," Angeline begged, her eyes full of tears. Her face was as white as a sheet and a sheen of sweat beaded her forehead. Exhausted, she crumpled into a heap on Bob's chest.

Bob lay perfectly still, looking from Toby to Angeline, who was now unconscious on his chest. He was equally startled and confused. People reached them from the landing above.

"Cover for her," Toby ordered under his breath, thinking quickly. "You fell but weren't hurt. You screamed because you were in shock." He lifted Angeline's limp body from his chest.

Bob nodded, agreeing to keep her secret.

"What happened?" a woman shouted as the first of

the crowd reached them and saw Bob.

"She tripped," Toby said, carrying her toward the passenger van.

"No," the woman protested. "I saw her. She didn't fall."

"She fell." Toby turned around and shot the woman a look of warning. "She hit her head."

"But . . ." The woman looked confused.

"She hit her head," Toby growled.

"She did," Bob offered weakly.

The woman turned her attention to Bob. "Are you all right?"

"Yeah, I was just in shock."

"But, I saw . . ." She furrowed her brow. "Your leg . . ."

"I'm fine." Bob sat up. "See?"

"But . . ."

"We're good." Bob's smile was uncertain. "She just got a bump on the head when she came to help me, that's all."

***

There was a commotion in the lobby, the likes of which had never been seen in the BOS Resort before. A rush of startled guests filtered into the lobby, following Angeline, who walked feebly, holding Toby's arm for support.

"I'm fine," she reassured them. "I just need to rest."

"If you have a concussion, you shouldn't sleep," Toby reminded her.

"Oh, right." She squeezed his arm gratefully.

Both Noah and Suna ran to meet them. "What happened?" Noah barked.

"She hit her head," Toby explained.

Noah took Angeline's arm from Toby and supported her weight. He looked into Toby's eyes and, for a split second, time stopped. Before he could form a coherent thought, Angeline's knees buckled beneath her, pulling him back into reality. He scooped her into his arms and walked her into one of the private consultation offices, casting glances over his shoulder at the man standing in the lobby. He was the brother Noah had been waiting to meet for the past three years.

CHAPTER TWENTY-EIGHT

Noah paced the room. Angeline was unconscious on the couch in the consultation room.

Suna placed her hand on his shoulder, compelling him to stand still.

"Does this mean that she knows?" he asked.

"Not necessarily," Suna answered.

"She couldn't have possibly . . ." Noah breathed.

"It's possible. A few of the kids I grew up with had similar abilities." Suna watched Angeline sleep sweetly on the couch. "But it takes decades to develop the kind of focus that allows you to . . ."

"Do you think that it could have been the vortex, or has she done this before?"

"I don't know," Suna answered.

Angeline's brow twitched infinitesimally. She was

pulled back into a state of semi-consciousness, but couldn't open her eyes because her lids felt like they had weights tied to them.

"Bob says that she hit her head, but fifteen other people said they saw her . . ." He shook his head and began to pace again. "What reason could Bob possibly have to lie? It doesn't make sense."

"Maybe he couldn't rationalize what happened . . ." Suna sat on the couch beside Angeline and touched her brow with the back of her hand to feel her temperature.

Angeline stirred and opened her eyes slightly. "Did they tell?" she whispered.

"Tell what, dear?" Suna asked gently.

"My secret," she asked quietly.

Suna and Noah's eyes met.

"What secret, darling?" Suna asked.

"The gold dust," Angeline said through the haze of drowsiness.

"What gold dust?" Noah spoke smoothly as to not rouse her further.

"The dust . . ." Angeline yawned.

Suna turned her head toward Noah. "I think she's dreaming." She touched Angeline's brow again, and she muttered something that couldn't be understood. "Can you get her a glass of water?"

"I'll be right back." Noah stepped out of the room.

"Angeline?" Suna shook her shoulder.

When Angeline opened her eyes and saw Suna's face, she smiled. She wasn't certain if this was a dream or real.

"I know," Suna said, looking deep into her eyes.

"Know what?" Angeline realized that she was no longer dreaming.

"Your secret."

"What secret?" Angeline eyed the room to locate Toby or Bob. They were nowhere to be found.

"It's okay," Suna promised. "I have a secret of my own. Would you like to hear it?"

***

Some secrets are best left unknown. Angeline strode along the side of the creek. Cathedral Rock, the most photographed land formation in Sedona, was on her right. One of the locals had told her that the vortex at Cathedral helped integrate all lives: past, present, and future.

Who am I?

What am I?

Upon Angeline's awakening from her post-healing delirium, Suna had pointed to a painting that hung on the wall, asking Angeline to look closely. It was one of the paintings that Allison had completed. A goddess held the world, a moon upon her forehead and the stars adorning her hair. When Angeline looked closely, she saw her face.

Suna had explained that she was, or rather, could be, the incarnation of Mother Earth. But it didn't make sense. If she was, wouldn't she have known? There was no way she could have possibly been someone as important as the Mother of the Earth . . . she couldn't even balance her checkbook, for goodness sake. She laughed violently. When she realized that she was cackling like a crazy person, she stopped.

Her feet carried her into the creek. She sloshed through the water as she walked upstream. The cool water did little to pull her back into the present as her mind spun in wild and unending circuits of thought.

"Who am I?" she whispered to the sky.

"What am I?" She pounded her feet into the riverbed.

"Answer me!" she called desperately to her soul.

Her foot slipped on a moss-covered rock. She fell into the water with a splash and was pulled downstream by the powerful monsoon season current. She struggled to keep her head above the water but was pulled under by the tow. Every single emotion that she had denied in the past and every slight that she had swept under the rug came rushing out at once, crashing over her with the same force as the current.

She wasn't only fighting the rough waters, but also all of the dark moments of her life. They rushed back in a flash of images, every disappointment, every angry face that she encountered, every sin that she ignored in the name of her own goodness. The more injustices she recalled, the harder she swam. She was so angry that if these flash of images were a precursor to death, she welcomed it.

Halfway upstream, the current broke, and she reached a gentler part of the river. Her own field of awareness softened, and she remembered all of the joys from her life and every tender fingerprint that had been left on her heart. A warm sensation filled her chest, like the hands of God caressing her lungs and radiating the golden fires of life directly into her heart. She stopped fighting the current and allowed herself to float, feeling completely revitalized. Her heart filled with such a grand sense of love that her body could hardly contain it. Hot tears ran from her eyes, falling into the water. She understood everything.

She saw humanity as if she were looking at them from the perspective of both heaven and Earth and they were precious, just like children. She understood that, like children going through the tumultuous process of adolescence, every human has to evolve in his or her own way, in his or her own time—so heaven patiently watched and Earth patiently endured the mindless destruction with the hope that one day humanity would remember their love for each other, as well as their gratitude for the celestial parents from which they were forged. All time and effort was offered in the quest for unity. She loved humanity, as if she were heaven, as if she were the Earth. And she could see how easy it would be for them to be happy if they just opened themselves to the love that was all around them. The love in the sky, the love from the Earth, even the love from within. They were surrounded by a sea of love, but were so keyed into each other that they missed it.

Angeline felt herself transform. She watched herself, as if from above, change into the Mother of the Earth. She felt the soul of the Earth fill her heart, and she knew that she had been reunited with her truest essence. This was why she was born. Every moment leading up to this made sense. Of course, she intuitively tried to heal anyone who was open to receive. She was a vessel, programed from birth, to one day embody the essence of original Mother.

She had fought that intuitive process because she didn't realize that this healing was her sole purpose on the Earth. She had mistakenly assumed that she must live by the same guiding principles of those around her, another cog in the machine, but that wasn't her destiny. Her only job on this Earth was to love the weary soul of each human being that she encountered until they were fully restored. Gone were the days of worrying about what job she could get or how much money she could squirrel away. Those concerns seemed so small to her now. Her job was to love.

Her perception expanded far and wide. She felt her mountains and valleys, her rainforests and deserts, she felt the entire surface of the Earth as if it were her own flesh. She admired the pristine beauty as if looking in the mirror. Pulled into a deep trance, she viewed the entire field of the Earth. From space, it looked like the golden aura surrounding a Buddha.

Love echoed through her every cell and filled her very being. It was warm, and it was safe; it was soft, and it filled her until she trembled. She felt the Earth tremble in unison. She was the voice of the Earth and the avatar of Mother Mago.

She heard a loud splash, felt a wave crash over her face. She coughed, pulled out of her floating water trance. A strong arm wrapped around her waist and towed her through the water.

CHAPTER TWENTY-NINE

"What are you doing?" Angeline pushed against the gladiator who had scooped her out of the water.

"I save you." He set her gently on the red stone landing and tapped his chest proudly.

She laughed. He was precious, a big burly man dripping in water, looking for a woman to save. She dare not break the news that she hadn't needed saving. She didn't want to ruin his moment.

"You are very brave." When she spoke, she felt a power she had never experienced before. Her voice was no longer just her voice. It moved the ether around them like she was talking through a bull horn.

He blushed, not because she called him brave, but because her saying so made him *feel* brave, noble, and righteous. He had aimed to be those things all of his life but had never felt them pound through his body. She spoke them into awareness.

"What is your name?" Her eyes softened.

"Leuters." He tapped his chest once more.

She shivered. Looking at the sky revealed that the sun had set. Leuters reached for his army-green satchel and pulled out a worn brown hoodie. He wrapped it around her shoulders and pulled the hood over her head. It was at least five sizes too big.

She clutched the fabric close to her small frame. She sat in the center of a powerful field of love, yet her heart still ached profoundly. For most of her life, her heart had resonated at a low-level ache, a result of feeling that life took too much from her. The ache that she experienced now was because she couldn't give enough, and it was a hundred times deeper. She wanted desperately to help everyone.

"You think funny." Leuters narrowed his eyes, trying to puzzle something out.

"Excuse me?" she asked.

"I ache, too," he confessed.

When she looked at his face, she saw his spirit shining through. His tanned face seemed to emit a soft white glow. He was a beautiful human being. She touched his heart with her palm. "Why do you ache?"

"People slaves. Just like before. Nobody know."

A shiver went through her whole body, but it wasn't due to the chill in the night air. She remembered him, though she didn't know how or why. She sensed that once upon a time he held an unspeakable preciousness to her.

"You know me?" he answered her thought.

"How do you do that?" she asked.

He pulled a bronze sword, blackened with ash, from his pack and put it into her hands. A memory flashed. She saw herself giving this bronze sword to him in another time, another place. She bestowed it upon him like a queen to a warrior. And then she was back.

"What is this?"

"Inheritance."

"Where did you get it?"

"Father." He pulled up his pant leg and revealed a prosthetic device.

"Did the sword do this to you?" She touched the metal of the weapon.

"Became one with sword."

"Did you do this to yourself?"

"Brother."

Another flash. She saw two brothers from a tribe long ago. A name came to her, "Jiso?" she breathed.

Leuters shook his head. "Alexandro."

"Do you have a picture of Alexandro?"

Leuters reached into his pack. A bundle of papers were bound together by a rubber band. He pulled out a picture and handed it to her. It was the man she had seen in her vision. *Jiso.*

Confusion twisted his features. "Your mind different," he said.

"It was a memory."

"When?"

"I don't know." She handed the photo back. "I don't understand."

"You remember me?"

"I think I do."

He looked into the distance for a long while. Angeline's body quivered with cold.

"I take you home," he said at last.

"I drove."

"I take you to protect."

"I assure you that I'm not in any danger," she laughed.

"You . . ." He tried to define his feelings with words. "You gentle soul."

"And you are a gentle man." She patted his hand. "I will drive myself, but if you want to follow me, we can have dinner. I want to hear all about you."

He nodded his head. "I follow you."

She had heard this vow spoken a very long time ago from the very same man.

I will follow you. I will protect you.

It was an echo from the past.

CHAPTER THIRTY

"You live here?" Leuters asked Angeline, eyeing the grounds of the BOS Resort. He was impressed, but not because it was a luxury estate. He could feel the intention of the community.

"I do." She opened the entrance door for him.

"Peace-filled," he said.

"Very peaceful," Angeline affirmed. The pristine lobby was filled with people. When they entered the room, conversations paused and curious glances rested upon them.

"They surprised by you." Leuters laughed heartily.

She shifted her head down and watched her feet as they walked.

"Hold head high," Leuters whispered, touching her shoulder. He understood what it felt like to be scrutinized by the public.

"I just . . ." She paused. "I'm not really comfortable with any extra attention."

"They focus on you till they have reason to focus on self." He touched her elbow. "Give them reason."

Angeline took a breath and placed the most dynamic smile on her face that she could manage. She greeted each person by name as they passed, pretending as if this moment were no different than any other. This informality seemed to put the occupants of the room at ease.

"Toby!" Angeline breathed a sigh of relief when she saw him. She leaned in for a hug. Once again, all eyes were on them.

"Where have you been?" He tucked a damp golden curl behind her ear. "And why are you wet?"

"I fell into the creek," she explained.

He noticed that a man stood with her. He turned to introduce himself and was almost struck speechless. "Leuters?"

"Toby." Leuters smiled, not at all surprised that their paths had crossed a second time.

"What are you doing here?" Toby looked to Angeline for an explanation. "Do you know each other?"

"Flow lead to destiny," Leuters repeated, the very

phrase he had spoken after meeting Toby.

"He sort of saved me from drowning," Angeline explained, knowing that it was a half-truth. Toby read her forehead. Leuters heard Toby's thought. They both looked at Angeline. She laughed. "What?"

"She no know?" Leuters asked Toby.

"Know what?" Angeline asked.

Suna approached them with quick steps, "Angeline, you had us worried."

"I'm sorry," she apologized. "I needed some time to think."

"That's understandable," Suna said. "But you just disappeared after . . ." She didn't finish the sentence, aware that they were under careful observation. "Next time, just let me know if you need anything."

"I will," Angeline promised.

Noah rushed into the lobby, out of breath. His eyes scanned the room, Angeline, Suna, and Toby stood with a tall Hispanic man who was as thick as a hundred-year-old oak tree.

"Angeline," he huffed. Leuters turned around, Noah recognized him. He had seen him three years ago while looking into Mago's soul. His eyes flitted to Suna. "Let's take this somewhere a little more private, shall we?"

They sat around the mahogany conference table in

the meeting room. A heavy silence hung in the air.

"I have a story to tell you," Noah began. "Three and a half years ago, I came to Sedona and had an awakening." He relayed the entirety of his experience on Bell Rock, where he met the soul of the Earth for the first time. Angeline leaned forward, listening as if hearing the story of her early life imparted by a parent.

"She said that when the time was right, I would meet all of you," Noah explained.

"Why?" Toby asked. He read Noah's thoughts but still didn't believe him. Experience had taught him that a crazy person believed their perceived reality wholeheartedly. Thoughts weren't always true.

"Because a very long time ago, each of us made a vow," Noah said.

Leuters leaned forward attentively. "What was vow?"

"To restore humanity to its original integrity," Suna answered.

"And how are we supposed to do that?" Toby asked with a caustic chuckle.

"By remembering who we are," Noah interjected.

"And who exactly are we?" Toby raised an eyebrow.

"God," Angeline breathed, recalling a flash of awareness that she had intuited during her experience in the river.

Toby laughed. He looked around the table. "You're not serious, are you?"

"What she said isn't untrue." Suna touched Toby's forearm.

"You mean to tell me that you think that the five of us," Toby motioned around the table, "are God? If that's the case, then why can't I manifest a cup of coffee right now?"

"Toby," Angeline's voice dropped in warning.

"You misunderstand," Suna explained. "What I'm saying is that all of us, every person on the planet, is God."

"You've got to be kidding." Toby stood up from the table. "I've had just about enough of this nonsense."

"Sit," Leuters barked, pulling Toby back into his chair.

"Toby," Angeline implored. "Please, just listen."

Their eyes met, and he softened. Against his better judgment he conceded, "I'll stay, but only because of her." He pointed to Angeline.

"You always were the difficult one." Suna shook her head affectionately. She wasn't discouraged by Toby's resistance in the least.

"And by *always*, you mean back when I was God?" Toby's eyes narrowed.

"You aren't *the* God," Suna explained patiently. "We

are all *aspects* of the God. And yes, you have lived many times before this one, during which we were connected. We are from the same soul family. Your true name isn't Toby, it is Chunggung."

"Chunggung?" he asked, disbelieving.

"Yes, and you are my brother."

"And why don't I remember this, but you do?"

"While you may have an extraordinary ability, you haven't awakened your consciousness yet."

This admission caught Toby's attention. "And what special ability might that be?"

"Read my mind," Suna challenged.

Toby and Leuters laughed.

"If my superpower is to be a pain in your neck, what's his?" He motioned toward Leuters.

"He is a medicinal alchemist," Suna answered.

Leuters shook his head, not understanding the term.

"Medicine man," Toby explained.

Leuters rubbed his chin. He'd never met this woman, but she'd hit the nail on the head. He'd turned his back on Western medicine after discovering that MFS was more effective for restoring health than the many medications he had prescribed while a doctor. "What my name?"

"Heak-So. And you were always my favorite. So

agreeable." She smiled.

"How long ago did we live?" Angeline asked.

"You came from a time before us. There is no way for me to know how long before. Time was experienced differently back then," Suna answered. "The four of us," she motioned around the table, "were created at the origin of our species. Things have changed so much since then."

"How so?" Angeline leaned forward.

"Everything was different. The condition of humanity was untouched by any selfish motivations. There was an innate sense of purity because everyone carried something called *the law* within them," Suna explained.

"What was *the law*?" Angeline asked.

"It wasn't one thing in particular," Suna said. "It was everything. The word 'law' had a completely different connotation back then. The modern day world has many laws, which are external rules of order enforced by threat of incarceration or penalty. But back then, it simply meant an intuitive connection to the whole. There was no separation between self and other. There were nations, as there are today, but everyone identified themselves simply as a citizen of the whole. There was abundance because we contributed wholeheartedly and had the power to manifest our intentions easily. Things weren't difficult, as they are today. There was no push and pull, no struggle. Everything flowed. We were able to communicate telepathically and teleport because there was no separation between heaven, the Earth, and all living beings."

"What happened?" Angeline breathed.

"Density," she said. "Back then, our bodies didn't have the density that they do now. We could have form if we chose, but essentially we are light bodies made of energy. Much like you would imagine an angel to be."

Toby sat back in his chair, undecided if he was willing to take the tale at face value. He resolved to listen, nonetheless.

"There was a young village boy named Jiso," Suna said.

"Wait," Angeline interrupted. "Did you say Jiso?"

She shot a glance to Leuters.

"Yes," Suna answered.

"Jiso," Angeline repeated the name to Leuters.

His heart beat rapidly. He reached into his canvas satchel and retrieved the picture that he had shown to Angeline earlier that day, handing it to Suna.

"He's here," Suna breathed, handing the picture to Noah.

"I don't believe it," Noah said, examining the picture.

"But he never took the vow," Suna said.

"He must've taken a vow of his own," Noah speculated. He turned to Leuters. "He was from your tribe."

"Tribe?" Leuters asked.

"Each of us," Suna motioned to everyone, except Angeline, "was responsible for the four original tribes of the Earth. Jiso was a member of your community," she explained. "How do you know him in this life?"

"Brother," Leuters said.

"Why is this important?" Angeline asked.

"Because Jiso was the first person to break the law," Suna said. "He was the one who created the illusion of separation."

CHAPTER THIRTY-ONE

There was no moon, but the stars shone like diamonds. The five climbed Bell Rock with a heightened sense of purpose. Tonight they would attempt to access the Crystal Palace to meet with the soul of the Earth together. Angeline trembled as she made the climb. She wasn't sure how she felt at the prospect of meeting the Being from whom she was forged. She teetered between excitement, nervousness and trepidation.

She wouldn't have believed any of what Suna and Noah had professed, except her vision at Cathedral Rock had shown her, specifically, how it was possible for her, a human being, to also be the Mother of the Earth. Deep within her brainstem, a drop of the purest divinity existed. It wasn't a generalized divinity either, but an intentionally placed seed direct from the essence of her oversoul, Mother Mago. The Mother of the Earth had chosen her, while she was still forming in her mother's womb, to be the vessel for her reemergence into the physical world. Mago was as much a part of her as her own mother, father, and even as much a part of her as her own soul.

Toby stumbled, cursing, as he slipped down the rock wall they climbed. Noah and Suna both took great care helping Angeline along the more challenging portions of the climb and surprisingly, Leuters did better than them all, despite his prosthetic leg.

"Angeline, please stand in the center," Suna directed, once they had reached the top. "Noah, Toby, Leuters and I will form a circle around you."

Awareness heightened, a circuit of energy flowed around the circle, breaking only when it reached Toby, the weak link in the chain.

Suna called direct attention to the disruption. "Toby, may I ask you why you have decided to come here with us?"

"I'm here for her," Toby said.

"So you did come willingly?"

"Yes," he said.

"Please actively suspend judgment then," Suna advised. "You'll find out soon enough if your skepticism is warranted. Until that moment comes, allow yourself the experience without resistance. We need you, *she needs you*, in order for this to work."

"Why?" he asked.

"We each have a gift that, when combined, will gain us entry into the Crystal Palace. The mind of Mago sees everything and is fooled by nothing. Energy does not lie. We each must contribute our utmost sincerity for this to work. "

Toby nodded. "I'll try."

"Will everyone around the circle please hold hands? We'll chant the ChunBuKyung. If you do not know the text, follow as best as you can," Suna said.

They began to chant. Within moments, Toby felt heat emanating from the mirror in his suit jacket pocket, just as he had the night the voice told him to come to Sedona. He looked down. Sunlight shimmered through fabric.

The pendant around Noah's neck also came to life, illuminating his face from below.

The sword on Leuters's forehead, previously only seen by Toby, was visible to everyone.

Suna's brass bell, which she had tucked into her cardigan pocket, also shone.

The seed of divinity within Angeline's brainstem lit

up, shining through her forehead and scalp, creating an aqua halo around her head.

The light generated among the five of them illuminated the top of Bell Rock, as if the moon were full on this dark night.

With every recitation, their pendants, talismans and medallions created a collective resonance, shifting the dimensions until their bodies had lost all density. They were quite literally made of light. Bell Rock shifted in unison. It quivered beneath their feet, more like a Jell-O mold than solid rock. The lines of the butte began to tremble and wiggle until it had swallowed them. And, just as Noah once had been, they were transported into the Crystal Palace within.

The cavern felt holy, like a church of the Earth. It was three stories high and supported by aquamarine columns, with sparkling geodes shaped exactly like the natural landscapes of Sedona.

"Now do you believe me?" Suna asked Toby.

His face softened with understanding. After being ejected from every household that he had known, for the first time, he felt at home. Overcome with emotion, he fell to his knees and touched the Earth with his fingertips. He closed his eyes for a moment, allowing himself to fully absorb the sensation of this homecoming.

"Is she here?" he asked, looking about the room.

Noah stepped into the center of the space and rested his palm on the crystal orb that held the essence of Mago's soul. When his hand touched its transparent surface, the aquamarine contained within beamed a column of light into the room from the top of the orb, creating a magnificent aqua bow of light that extended from the orb to the other side of the room.

"My most beloved children . . ." Angeline spoke in a voice that was not her own.

Everyone in the room turned, prompted by the change in her voice. She sat atop the diamond Cathedral Rock, Mago's throne. The aqua light funneled into the top of her head; her eyes shone bluer than the ocean. They seemed to be lit from within.

"Mago?" Toby breathed.

"It's me," she said. It was the same maternal voice that had spoken to him his last night in New York.

It's not your fault, it had said. *All of the things that you have done were part of a destined process. You are a great man. More than anyone, you are a rare and precious gem. It is time to remember your true identity.*

"Chunggung," he whispered his name. "I remember." He dropped his head into his hands.

"Why do you cry, Chunggung?" Mago asked.

"Because . . . ." He couldn't get the words out.

"Are these tears of sorrow or tears of joy?"

"Both," he cried. "I remember the joy, the fullness of knowing you. And yet my heart breaks under the weight of my shame."

"Why are you ashamed?" Her soft voice echoed through the cavern.

"I don't want you to see what they did to me, what I've turned into," he admitted. He could sense how greatly he had been tainted. "And I don't want you to see what I've done," he sobbed. "I couldn't keep my purity, the law. It was too hard. I just couldn't . . ."

She rose from her throne, kneeled beside him and wrapped her arms around him maternally. He lamented his difficult life, the boy who had endured the death of his mother, the abuse of his father, and a life of unchecked excess. She whispered into his ear, "You made it. You suffered, almost more than your soul could bear, but you made it." She stroked his hair. "I will give your soul wings again."

"If you knew what I've done," he cried.

"I have felt everything that you have done and everything that has happened to you. I was with you," she said. "You mustn't look behind you, there is so much more to come. We are together now."

He looked into Angeline's eyes, yet it wasn't Angeline. It was *her*. The one person he'd waited to meet his whole life. "I know that I've just met you. That I forgot everything. But now that I've found you, I feel how empty my life was without you."

"I've felt empty, too. My heart has been broken for thousands of years."

"You've had a broken heart?" Toby cried, for this perfect being embodied the very essence of love.

"I am very tired, my son." She touched his cheek.

"Why?" he asked.

"This world is exhausting. Your sorrow is my sorrow. Every child's hunger is my own. Each abuse inflicted over the resources that I offer freely is my lament. I feel every single pain experienced upon this Earth. I see everything, I feel everything and still I can't understand why the world has come to this. My children's hearts have turned to stone." She looked into Toby's eyes. "And it's my fault." A tear slipped down her cheek.

"How can it be your fault?" Leuters asked, speaking in Spanish and resting his palm on her shoulder. All of her children gathered to sit around her, touching her arm, leaning on her shoulder, folding bodies down to rest in her lap.

"I created you. I created the world. I poured so much

love into my creation, but I overlooked one small detail. It was a flaw that couldn't be fixed without destroying everything and starting from the beginning," she said. "And I just couldn't do it. That's why I've let things progress as far as they have. I couldn't bear to destroy my children."

"So you have endured us destroying you?"

"And each other," she cried.

"What happened?" Noah asked. "What was the flaw?"

"A single desire," she said. "It was just a simple little desire, so small, that led to eons of death and destruction. And for you, my precious souls, the darkness has just begun. All of the darkness that exists in the world will soon be yours to bear," she warned, her eyes filled with fresh tears.

"Will you tell the story, Mago?" Noah asked. She had previously shared it with him, but he felt that it was important that the others hear it from her directly.

She nodded her head. "It all started with a young village boy named Jiso . . ."

CHAPTER THIRTY-TWO

Jiso had just finished his duties in the village. The community had expanded so quickly that each day his work led him further from the center of town. His chosen profession was an artist. He beautified the village by infusing the flora with energy. The plant life grew without his assistance, of course. However, with his aid, the flowers bloomed brighter, the stalks grew longer and the pollen burst from the center like fireworks. He spent hours a day walking the village, drawing upon the golden aura that surrounded him and channeling its radiance into the landscape, plant by plant.

He knew that he should have headed back to town hours ago, but he was too enraptured by his last task to consider the diminishing strength of his aura. The family of his prospective life-companion was to move to a plot of land nearby, and he wanted Nia to witness the most magnificent show of color from the bedroom window of their new home. It was a labor of the truest love.

He felt light, as if any moment he would disappear. The nearest fountain was only fifty feet away. He would recharge his aura by drinking the *milk of the Earth* that flowed from the spring, the essence of Mago herself. These fountains ran along the meridians of the Earth, and sprung up where the gridlines crossed. He had never tasted the milk this far from his home and was curious what hint it would carry—the river, the field, the honeysuckle-colored Earth. Each spring was imbued with the essence of the land from which it sprung. He licked his lips. Thinking about it made him that much more thirsty.

Jiso tapped his foot, looking ahead in line. There were five people in front of him. He felt impatient because his life force had depleted more than it ever had before. The line in front of him suddenly broke, and the people scattered.

"What's going on?" he asked a woman who passed.

"The well ran dry," she explained.

"Ran dry?" He had never heard of such a thing.

"Yes, they think something may have dammed the flow. There is another well two hundred feet that way," she offered, raising a finger to point.

"Er, thanks." Jiso turned his head in that direction.

"You are most welcome. See you there."

Jiso felt weak. He sat on the edge of the empty well and tried to gather strength. He'd waited too long to reconnect with the Earth, assuming that he could pop by the well and replenish himself easily. But now, he was uncertain that he'd make it to the next well. He closed his eyes. Waves of light passed through his mind.

"I can do this," he breathed.

Another wave of light passed through his consciousness when he stood, causing him to faint.

When he awoke, the sun had set. He tried to teleport himself, but didn't have enough power. He tried to push himself up, but didn't have enough density. He looked around, searching for someone, anyone, who could help him. The night was quiet.

He took notice of a grapevine that grew along the base of the well, one that he'd previously infused with the essence of his aura. It glimmered and shimmered with life in the moonlight. He reached his fingers forward and tried to pluck a plump grape from the vine, but his fingers passed through it. He focused his attention, channeling the remaining energy distributed throughout his body into his fingertips and pulled again. The grape popped free.

"I honor you," he said. "I have imbued you with my life force and now I request that I may borrow it back." He popped the grape into his mouth and bit down, uncertain if his plan would work.

"Oh, my God," he breathed as his teeth broke the thin skin of the grape and its essence poured into his mouth. A tidal wave of moisture, imbued with the power of life, burst forth, stroking his tongue. His entire field of awareness drew into a singular point: the sensation of the grape in his mouth. His body shivered in ecstasy.

"All of the power contained in heaven and Earth is within this single grape," he whispered, breathless. The grape was so small, and yet its power flooded all of his senses at once. Sensations unfamiliar to him exploded through his body; a rush of heat and the gathering of molecules ricocheted through his every single cell. He felt the strength of a thousand men and his sensory system heightened to excruciating levels of ecstasy. He could smell, see, taste, touch, and feel in a way he had never fathomed. He leapt to his feet, compelled to run, feeling that, if he stopped, this surge of unfathomable power would consume him.

When he awoke in the morning, he felt immense

guilt. He had ended the life of another living being. Intuitively, he knew that this went against the natural order of life. In order to dull the guilt that sliced through his soul, he tried to justify his actions. He resolved to never speak of it and never, ever, do it again.

As the weeks passed, he could think of nothing but the grape and the experience it had evoked. He was distracted, plagued by questions. Instead of communing with the mind of heaven and Earth, his mind began to speak with itself. He wondered if any of the other flora possessed the same power. With every plant he touched, he imagined what it would feel like in his body. He tried to control these thoughts, but they controlled him. He was obsessed.

As he infused a juniper tree with life force, curiosity got the better of him. He pulled one of the berries free.

"Jiso!" Nia called. "What are you doing?"

He turned quickly, clutching the berry tightly behind his back.

"Hi, Nia." He hoped that she didn't notice.

She did. "Jiso, why did you do that?"

"Do what?"

"Rip that berry off."

"I didn't."

"You did, I saw the tree tremble," she accused.

He knew he had been caught. He relayed the story of consuming the grape on the night that the well had run dry. "I was curious if the juniper would have a similar effect," he explained.

"But, Jiso." She looked around. "It's wrong."

"Who says it is wrong?" he asked.

"Well," she said hesitantly. "No one specifically, but it *feels* wrong."

"You should taste how delicious it is." He held the berry up between two fingers. "Try half?" he suggested, tearing half the berry off with his teeth.

"No." She looked from side to side, uncertain.

Jiso leaned forward and kissed her. The berry's juice zinged on her tongue. She pulled back from his embrace and looked into his eyes, startled. He kissed her again, with a passion that they had never experienced before. He fed her the remaining half of the berry, and the two of them made love under the juniper tree, feeling every ridge, sensation and touch. A whole new dimension of perception opened to them both, a kaleidoscope of senses, and they were transfixed.

CHAPTER THIRTY-THREE

"I always knew that, as the population grew, my children would graduate from drinking the milk. It was expected," Mago explained. "The fact that Jiso fell into the experience with abandon, treated it like a drug, was unexpected," she said. "He lost his mind."

"You mean he went crazy?" Suna asked.

"He let himself become intoxicated. His mind followed the sensations the grape heightened: taste, touch, smell, sex and sound, which are fleeting." She paused and turned to Toby. The tone of her voice left little room for doubt that the moral of this story applied directly to him. "He had to find more, something new to consume, something new to chase, always looking outside of himself for more stimulation. If he'd just managed the sensations, observing them as they passed through his body without being swept away," she said. "If he'd handled the situation with a certain maturity, then the world would have progressed very differently. There would be no corruption, and there wouldn't be such an unhealthy imbalance of ego."

"That was so long ago. Jiso couldn't possibly be responsible for the world that we live in today." Leuters spoke in Spanish and once again, everyone understood. In this dimension, there was no difference in language. The mother tongue was understood telepathically.

"Jiso's eagerness to experience intoxication with Nia caused him to introduce the juniper berry to her in a certain way. It wasn't introduced as food; it was introduced as a drug. He stimulated her senses, then had sex with her under the juniper tree, without love, without respect. He consumed her, just as he had consumed the juniper berry, and a life-long pattern was set up for both of them."

"And when they introduced the flora with others, it was from the same mindset," Noah guessed.

"Precisely," Mago said. "These sensations were approached as something to gain and because people now had something outside of themselves that could be sought, greed entered the human psyche. People began to ignore the intuitive connection with the laws of the universe that existed within them while in pursuit of greater stimulation. The lines of right and wrong got blurrier and blurrier until life in Mago Castle, the name of our community, was tainted."

"Is that when the ego was born?" Noah asked.

"It was when the present moment was lost, re-placed by the need for more stimulation, more noise. So, if you consider the ego to be future-based, consumption-motivated consciousness, then yes. It was when the ego was born."

"I wish something could have been done to remedy the situation." Suna shook her head.

"You wished for that, even then. Your heart is so like mine." Mago touched her hand. "When harmony in the village broke down, it was you who came seeking a method of training to help manage the senses. You took what you learned and taught the people to develop their observer consciousness so that they wouldn't be swept away by sensations."

"But it didn't work?" Noah asked.

"Obviously not," Toby scoffed.

"For a time, it worked," Mago said. "But the addic-tive mindset proved difficult to break, and so many had already been enthralled by their senses."

"Why did you make the five senses based on

stimulation?" Leuters asked.

"It was meant as a gift," Mago said.

"That turned into a curse," Toby grumbled.

"You are missing the point," she said. "It's natural to enjoy sensation. However, in your case, Toby, the curse was your obsession with satisfying your sensory hunger. That wasn't my fault, the grape's fault, nor was it Jiso's. You behaved in ways that went against your nature. You flew around the world, had everything that money could buy, drank, did drugs, had sex with countless women."

"I did," Toby admitted, shocked by the reprimand.

"Was there a point, ever, that your soul overflowed with joy, or, at the very least, felt completely satisfied?" she pressed.

"Never," he answered, looking down. It was difficult to be seen so completely.

"It's a never-ending cycle, Toby. There's nothing outside of you that can replace what was intended to live inside of you."

"I did everything wrong."

"And because of that you missed what was intended for you." Mago softened. "The connection you were created to experience, the one that will nourish you beyond comprehension, is still possible. You just have to stop chasing after the next sensation long enough to give it space to grow."

"Give what space to grow?" He looked up.

"Your soul," she answered. "And its reinstatement with the law. The law is the key. Without it, your soul won't grow."

"Will you help me find it?" he pleaded.

"It already exists within you," she answered. "It's why you have come. The vow that you made was to return when the world was at its tipping point, access the law held in your spiritual DNA, and show others how to access it as well, which will restore the Earth to the one in which you were first born. That was your promise to me."

"The five of us?" Leuters looked around the circle. "Restore the law in every single member of humanity?"

"If one percent adopt the law, then it will reach a critical mass and become the culture. And of the one percent, you are only four million away from the tipping point. The people of your time are savvy, free thinkers who have finally become bored with consumption. They are ready to wake up and discover what it is like to truly live. It's an exciting time. A new era of abundance and contribution is possible within three years. However, I must warn you."

"What?" Noah asked.

"You will face many obstacles. The people are ready to be freed, but there are systems in place, people in positions of power who will fight the bearers of this change. The more light you bring to the world, the more darkness you will have to endure. I cannot make what you will face easier, but I can give you strength."

***

The five sat atop Bell Rock. "What happened?" Angeline blinked. It was dark. The last thing she remembered was the Crystal Palace. It was disorienting, being in one place, then without warning, another, with no recollection of how she got there.

"Mago?" Toby asked, trying to identify who he spoke to.

"It's me," Angeline said. "But I feel her in my heart."

"You don't remember?" Noah asked.

She looked around the group. "It's a little fuzzy. I remember Mago's essence coming through me, observing you through my eyes. I remember Toby crying, and wanting so much to help him." She touched his cheek. "And then I was here." She looked around the dark night and shivered.

Noah met Suna's eyes. Suna placed her hand

maternally on Angeline's shoulder. "Let's get you home and warm. We have a lot to discuss."

CHAPTER THIRTY-FOUR

"I'm going to share one of the first lessons that my teacher shared with me," Suna said.

After meeting the soul of Mago, they decided to meet at Boynton Canyon for training, to develop their senses. Suna, by far the most experienced, offered to lead the session. She began with light stretching to open the energy meridians of the body.

Leuters appeared to enjoy the stretching most. He moaned and groaned with pleasure as his stiff muscles softened and his circulation improved. He didn't seem bothered that Toby and Angeline snickered at his hearty vocalization. When they had finished the full routine, Suna called Angeline to stand with her at the front of the clearing.

"Angeline," she said. "Can you describe your gift

for us please?"

"Sometimes, I can exchange my health for another's illness."

"So, when you transfer energy to someone, it's an exchange rather than a gift?"

"I guess," she answered.

"And it's difficult for your body to recover?"

"Yeah," Angeline replied.

"The reason you experience this is because you are using your personal energy," Suna said. "It's important that all of us learn how to harness the universal energy available to us. I will call this energy LifeParticles, the purest particles of life. And it's these LifeParticles that will enable you to perform great feats of healing without taxing your personal reserves."

"How can I access them?" Angeline asked.

"You already know how, you just need to remember. Close your eyes and breathe in. Although you cannot see the air that your lungs gather, you feel it. Correct?"

Angeline nodded her head.

"It's the same with LifeParticles: though you may not be able to see them, they are all around you, waiting to respond to your thoughts and emotions. You already use them to create. The trick is to learn how to use them to create with intention."

"So, to use these LifeParticles to create what I wish, all I have to do is change my thoughts?"

"Yes," Suna answered. "I want you to practice imagining yourself standing in the very center of a sea of LifeParticles. See them trembling with responsiveness to your every thought. Befriend each and every little twinkling particle. Tell them your hopes and dreams. That will be a helpful first step in familiarizing yourself with the tools that are available to help you create what you hold dear to your heart."

"I will," Angeline promised.

"We will check back next week to hear your experiences. Thank you, Angeline." Suna touched her shoulder. "Leuters, please come forward."

Leuters limped to the front.

"And what is your gift?" Suna asked.

"I hear thought," Leuters said.

"Is that all?" Suna asked.

"Sometime I can rethink thought into person's brain. Like editor," he answered.

"So you can purify a person's thoughts?"

"Yes," Leuters answered.

"Leuters has an exceptional gift. If someone is stuck inside a negative thought loop, he has the ability to free them. People think that he's easy to be around because he is agreeable, but it's much more than that. Leuters's power is a perfect example of the third level of mastery that enables a person to shift from victim-consciousness to God-consciousness. Though his gift is special, we all possess this capability."

"How?" Noah asked.

"People talk about what is going on in their mind. Leuters has the ability to change a person's thought on a subconscious level, but we all have the power of the spoken word. If a person complains about being sick, tell them you can see they are on the road to wellness— and if you are sincere enough for them to believe you, you will have changed their destined path."

"How many levels of mastery are required to reach God-consciousness?" Angeline asked.

"Five," Suna replied.

"Five?" Angeline asked, in disbelief.

"Not as many as you imagined?"

"Not nearly," Angeline said. "Where did you learn about this?"

"From my teacher," Suna said. "He came up with a systemized approach to enlightenment that doesn't stem from a belief in a particular institution, but simply from the development of the human brain, since enlightenment is a function of the brain."

"How can I improve gift?" Leuters asked.

"Experience is the best teacher. Every time you hear a thought that doesn't empower the thinker to a higher state, correct it. The same goes for the rest of you: every time you hear someone misspeak, either against themselves, or others, gently pose another, brighter option," she suggested. "Toby, it's your turn. Will you come to the front?"

Leuters and Toby exchanged places.

"Toby, what's your gift?"

"I can read people's thoughts, but only when I hold this mirror that my grandmother gave me." He pulled the little bronze mirror out of his pocket.

"Are you sure about that?"

"Quite," he said.

"Will you give me the mirror?" she asked, holding out her palm.

Toby had never, in his life, let someone else hold his keepsake. He put it in her hand.

"Please look at the group," Suna directed.

Toby looked at Leuters, who smiled broadly. He saw the sword lighting up his forehead. He cast a quick glance at Angeline, whose encouraging thoughts streamed across her forehead.

"What?" Toby breathed.

"You no longer need a trinket. The power has been awakened within you." Suna handed the mirror back to him. "You can keep it if you like, because it has sentimental value, but it is no longer necessary. This week, I want you to stretch the boundaries of your talent by trying to read the group energy. Anytime that you see a group of three or more, try to read the collective thought."

"But groups don't have thoughts. Individuals have thoughts."

"I wouldn't be so sure about that," Suna said. "If you look at any group, really look, you can see that they all kind of look alike. Their energy patterns are similar. It's because they have tapped into a group consciousness."

"I'll try," he said, doubting.

"You need to do more than try. Mago told us that we need to affect a shift that brings one percent of the population into master consciousness. You are the one who can measure how close or how far we are. We need you to be able to tap into the mass consciousness of the Earth at any given time. It's important, Toby."

"I understand," he said.

"Noah, will you come to the front?" Suna asked.

"I'm not exactly sure what my gift is," he confessed, as he made his way to the front.

"You don't know it yet, but you have the inherent ability to recalibrate the realities that are stuck in people's chakras. Look at your medallion," Suna said. "As brilliantly as those chakra-colored gems shine, so will the chakras that you heal."

"What's your gift?" he asked.

"My gift is my voice. When I chant the ChunBuKyung I reach a pitch that resonates with the highest expression of LifeParticle energy and creates an interference pattern, or waves, through the ocean of them. Anyone in the vicinity is affected by those waves," she explained, "since the human body is also composed of LifeParticles."

They concluded the training by chanting the ChunBuKyung to first calibrate the particles of life in the ether around them, then practiced drawing the energy of the LifeParticles into their lower abdomens with deep breathing. By the end of the session their faces were gleaming with life. Noah had an epiphany. If accessing universal power was truly so simple, he could share the same techniques with everyone he met and influence a faster change on the Earth. It was almost too simple.

CHAPTER THIRTY-FIVE

The car ride was quiet. Each person was drawn into contemplation, replaying the events of the day. Toby considered the prospect of awakening the whole of humanity to hearing that small still voice within, the internal compass, and using it as a guiding system to live. It was a tall order. So many before them had tried, and failed.

Noah turned on his blinker. The sound of it echoed through the interior of the SUV. He pulled into the parking lot of the BOS Resort.

"Is this her?" Angeline heard a man's voice echo through the lobby as she entered. Multiple camera flashes blinded her, preventing her from seeing the owner of the voice.

"Excuse me." Noah pushed the camera away.

"What's this about?"

"Is she the one?" the cameraman asked, motioning for his counterpart to join them.

"The one, what?" Noah asked.

"The one who can heal like Christ," the cameraman replied.

"Excuse me?" Suna coughed. "Who are you?"

An attractive gentleman wearing a tan cashmere cardigan jogged toward them. "Hello," he said, holding his hand out for a shake. "I'm Jeremy Waters, with *Newsline*."

Leuters and Toby stepped in front of Angeline protectively.

"Hold on, fellas." Jeremy laughed. "I'm just investigating a story here. I heard that this woman," he flashed a disarming smile in Angeline's direction, "is quite special. And I am interested in getting to know her."

"For *Newsline*?" Noah confirmed. It was one of the highest-ranking news programs on television.

Jeremy smiled and nodded. Suna placed her hand on Noah's forearm and whispered in his ear, "This is exactly what we have been praying for."

Noah turned to Jeremy. "And how did you hear about us?"

"We got an email from someone who was on a hike

and saw . . . something miraculous," Jeremy answered.

Jeremy was in his late twenties and had an award-winning smile. His wide honey-colored eyes seemed to let the world in without filter. He looked trustworthy, like the boy next door.

A surge of energy, released from Angeline's brain stem, sent shivers down her spine. She felt the presence of Mago bloom within her, like a rose from a bud. She observed herself stepping forward and smiling, uncertain if it was her or Mago who spoke.

"Hello." She offered her hand. "I'm Angeline."

"Jeremy," he replied, placing his palm in hers. Angeline felt a surge of golden energy release from her heart and move through her arm into his hand. Her golden aura, previously only reserved for the sick, enveloped him. He relaxed instantly.

"Did you want to speak with me?" she asked.

"Oh yes," he said, entranced by the sensation of love that now wrapped him like a warm blanket. He felt a twirling heat in his abdomen, and his hands became warm and moist. He instantly felt healthy. Life energy circulated through him like it had at his peak, a teen-ager playing high school football. He could have done a hundred pushups without breaking a sweat.

"I think that perhaps we should speak in private,

first," Angeline suggested. "To answer your questions." She looked deeply into his eyes. "I can see how bored you are with life," she said, reading the energy of his soul. "You are a big, bright, dynamic star in the midst of a gray, monotone world. You have a mission, a greater purpose for your life. If you are interested, I would like to share with you what I see."

"I would like that very much," he said, transfixed.

Angeline turned to her friends. "Suna, may we use your consultation room?"

"Of course," Suna answered. "Jeremy, can I offer you a cup of tea?"

"Yes, thank you." He turned to his camera-man. "Doug, can you get some footage of the resort for the B roll?"

"Sure thing, Jeremy," he answered, picking up his camera and resting it on his shoulder. "Want me to get interviews with the guests and employees as well?"

Jeremy cast a glance to Noah, who gave a nod of consent. "Please do."

***

"Should we just let her talk to him like that?" Toby shifted his foot onto the coffee table. He was irritated.

He looked at his watch. "They've been in there

over an hour."

"Can't control world," Leuters said, placing his hand on Toby's shoulder. "Have to trust."

"Yeah, but, we have no idea what he's asking her in there. He could be trying to trick her into saying something that could—" Toby could only imagine the possibilities. He rubbed his face in frustration. "She could be telling him—this is *not* a good idea."

"She special," Leuters said. "World should know."

"I don't trust the world," Toby grumbled. "He compared her to Christ, for God's sake. They are going to crucify her, too."

"She not claiming to be Christ," Leuters assured him. "Only herself."

Toby cast a sideways glance. Leuters obviously didn't place any stock in his acutely realistic concerns. "I'm gonna talk to Noah about this."

Toby kicked his feet off the table and lifted himself from the lobby couch, striding to Noah's office. He walked in without knocking. Noah looked up.

"You aren't worried about this?" Toby exclaimed, motioning to the closed consultation door.

Noah shook his head. "No."

Toby turned to Suna, in search of an ally. She laughed, walking across the office to rest her hand on his shoulder. "You worry too much. This is a good thing. We can't put all of our efforts into saving the world and have no one know about it." A wry smile passed her lips. "Eventually, it is bound to get out."

"Not you, too," Toby groaned. "Am I the only sane, logical person who didn't happen to fall off the turnip truck yesterday?"

"Have a little faith," Suna chuckled.

"This is a bad idea," Toby moaned. He had an uncomfortable feeling in his gut. Something wasn't right; he was certain of it. He calmed himself by resolving to use his resources and connections to squash this story before it aired. He would trade every favor, pay any amount, to protect her.

***

Angeline invited Jeremy to sit on the yoga mat on the floor. They sat facing each other, with crossed legs, sipping tea from tiny Asian cups. Angeline set her cup on the floor. Her movements were intentional and precise. She leaned forward and touched his knee. "Do you recognize me?"

"You. I feel like I remember you, though I am certain we have never met." He stumbled over his words.

"Right now, we are in a moment at the center of eternity," she said. "All past, all future is overlapping in this present moment. That's why you feel as if you remember me. Because you are fully present in this moment, and the moment is eternal. You will help me a great deal, though there will be a time when it will appear that coming to meet me was a mistake. What I will encounter because of this meeting will upset you. When what is to come arrives, I want you to remember that I chose it. It's not your fault. Even before coming to this place, as this girl, in this body, I chose my fate."

"I don't understand," he said.

She took his hands. "You will."

"Is it true?" he asked. "Are you like the Christ?"

"I am only myself," Angeline laughed. "The Christ came with a message of another world, a heaven to attain after death. I have come with a message of *this* world, a message that points to a state of heaven to be attained while still on Earth. I don't think we should have to leave this planet to be happy."

CHAPTER THIRTY-SIX

"I've called this meeting because we need a strategy," Noah said. Since the original airing of the *Dateline* interview the BOS Resort had been flooded with more visitors than they knew what to do with. Each employee was working around the clock to keep up with the lectures, private sessions and varying inquiries.

"According to Mago, we only have four million more people to enlighten, and we have three years to do it. We need to make a serious plan to accomplish that."

"So busy," Leuters said.

"Yeah," Angeline agreed. "I don't see how we can take much more on. Even if we could, the resort just doesn't have the room available. We are at capacity as it is."

"How many people visit the resort on average per week?" Noah asked Toby, who had taken over the revenue projections.

"About one thousand," he answered.

"If we wake up one thousand people each week for the next three years, that's only one and a half million. Less than half of the number of lives that need to be impacted by a greater value system. Even if we work ourselves to the bone, it's not enough."

"What are you thinking?" Suna asked.

"We need to go online," Noah proposed.

"A website?" Toby protested.

"Not just a website, a cyber-university. Somewhere anyone, around the globe, can go to connect to an energy greater than their own, drinking in all the inspiration required to make changes in their daily lives. We can have videos of Suna and Angeline's lectures, mindful entertainment talk shows, natural cooking. Really, the sky is the limit. But we'll need help."

"We'll have to hire a new staff," Toby advised. "That would be something that I would be interested in investing in."

"Can I count on you to head up the project?" Noah asked.

"You can," Toby promised.

***

"A million hits in two days," Suna whistled.

Noah patted Leuters on the back and sat in the chair next to him.

"They say no make MFS. They not say no tell people about it," Leuters chuckled.

Leuters had recorded a video tutorial in his backyard on how to make a derivative of MFS using natural ingredients that could be easily obtained. He was careful to explain that the supplement wasn't meant for human consumption due to recent legislation, but cited the health benefits it promised if it were to ever become legal. He posted the video on their website, not expecting anything more than a marginal result, but something about it caught the interest of the public and within hours it went viral.

"That's more hits than Angeline's blog on *creating a business that makes your soul sing.*"

"Heh," Leuters laughed. He couldn't help but love the spotlight. It was blissfully warm. He had looked for many ways to contribute to the movement but always fell short, because he had tried to model what the others were doing. He hadn't realized that all he had to do was be himself and share what he had to offer.

"Welcome to the big leagues." Angeline stepped behind his chair and massaged his shoulders. "You're our breakout star," she laughed.

"Where are we on the Richter scale?" Noah asked Toby the question that he had asked at least once a week for the past two years.

"About two million more to go," Toby answered. "We are halfway there, and we have a year remaining."

"What were the total hits for the website last year?"

"A hundred million," Toby said, looking at his notebook.

Noah did the math in his head. "And what is the number of people who've been exposed to our programs, either online or at the wellness centers?"

"Worldwide?" Toby asked.

"Worldwide," Noah confirmed.

"Over three hundred million," Toby answered.

Noah exhaled, scrubbing his face with his palm. "And only two million additional people have become conscious since we started?"

"Yes," Toby answered.

Noah became serious. He wasn't in the mood to mince words. "If we are reaching three hundred million people—and only two million are making a measurable change—what we are doing isn't enough. It needs to be better. We need to be better." He looked each of them in the eye. "And nobody in this room is going to sleep tonight until we figure out what we are going to do differently."

CHAPTER THIRTY-SEVEN

"You are someone else's proof that God exists," Angeline explained to the audience in the recently opened BOS Resort in Los Angeles.

She and Suna spent most of their time traveling the globe, which consisted of midnight flights, early morning meet and greets and all-day lectures. Angeline's eyes were particularly blurry today, due to the combination of the late night and early morning, but she couldn't have been happier to see the 2,500 faces that looked back at her. She wished that Suna had been able to join her, but she was hosting a lecture of her own, in Germany.

"If you would only allow your natural consciousness to shine from you, uninterrupted, you would become living proof that the consciousness of God can exist through a human being. I'm talking to you, a regular human being, with regular worries. If you were to transcend all odds and stop engaging in the shit of the world, stop splashing around the gutter of your own subconscious for long enough to let your enlightened consciousness emerge, you would prove once and for all that human beings are made in God's image. Our whole history would be reframed. You would *make* history and change our future."

When Angeline had first arrived at the BOS Resort two years ago, penniless and broken-spirited, she never would have imagined that she would evolve into one of its keynote speakers. Since the airing of the *Dateline* special, thousands upon thousands of people had flocked to various BOS Resorts in search of healing. But it wasn't enough. The thought of all of the souls that she had yet to meet, literally, kept her up at night. Her heart ached to free the people of the world from the nightmare that society had created. Enlightenment was a choice. And she was going to educate as many people as she could about that choice.

She took her seat on the chair placed at the center of the stage. "There is nothing to learn, no scripture to memorize. There is nothing to place your faith in, nor is there anything to believe. There is only *one thing* that will lead you to your enlightenment: the experience of the divinity that already exists within you. You already have it. Raise your hand if you feel that you are worthy of enlightenment at this very moment."

A few hands rose. Most of the audience looked around to see who had raised their hand, uncomfortable at the prospect of claiming their worthiness. Angeline addressed one of the audience members, a gentleman in the third row.

"Are you absolutely certain that you are worthy, right now, for *enlightenment*?" she asked.

The man nodded his head in affirmation.

"What makes you worthy?" she asked, curious.

"I've spent the last twelve years pursuing it," he answered.

"Twelve years?" she whistled. "That is a long time."

"Yes, it is." he confirmed.

"*Twelve years of pursuit, in all of eternity*," she giggled. "You can work at a company for twenty-five years and all you'll get is a gold watch."

He shifted in his chair, seeming less certain of his declaration of worth.

"That's okay," she assured him. "It was a trick question to illustrate a point." Angeline felt the hairs along her body stand on end, and the stench of sulfur filled the room. When the pungent odor engulfed her, her skin burned as if she were standing in front of a sand blaster. She kept talking, despite the cloud of sulfur-scented sepia-tinted consciousness that threatened to overcome her. She knew, without a doubt, that this unseen force was trying to prevent her from speaking the next words.

"Enlightenment is not about worthiness; it's about willingness. You could spend eons trying to become worthy, but if you are willing, enlightenment can happen in a blink of an eye."

She called upon the spirit of Mago for help. She called upon the energy of heaven to engulf the room. Her mind reached in all directions, seeking a spiritual ally to help her clear the ether. Angeline heard the twinkle of Suna's brass bell. She looked around the auditorium. She heard it again.

"Er," Angeline paused, having lost focus. It couldn't have been any other bell, of that Angeline was certain. Suna's bell had a unique ting, celestial and delicate but also strong and clear. "You are here, which presumably means that you are interested in enlightenment. Fortunately, your quest is not in vain. You can walk out of this room today, fully awakened. The question isn't how worthy you are, but rather how *willing* are you to let go of everything that you think you know and learn a new way of being."

She breathed a sigh of relief when she felt the familiar texture of Suna's clear consciousness unfold around her. Though she was halfway around the globe, Suna had answered Angeline's call. Angeline continued the lecture, more determined than ever. "Many people want to become enlightened because they dream of a better job, better relationships, or more confidence." She looked around the auditorium, feeling every soul in the room. "The answer is, once you are enlightened, you have a better *everything*. There is no area of your life that this consciousness won't touch.

"If you have a dream of a better world, the change starts with you. And the change starts now. When you entered this room, your destiny changed. When you walk out of this room, the world will change," she said.

CHAPTER THIRTY-EIGHT

"The conference in San Diego conflicts with the event in Dallas on the twenty-third of this month." Noah adjusted his reading glasses. "I'm thinking that if Suna handles the lecture in San Diego, then she can fly into Dallas on the twenty-fourth and catch the second day of filming." He looked up.

"Why is it important that we are all there?" Toby asked.

"Because Jeremy will be there for the follow-up interview. We should all be on hand in case he wants to speak with any of us."

"Cancel San Diego?" Leuters asked.

"The event sold out months ago. We should honor our agreement," Noah said.

"I need Suna with me in Dallas both days,"

Angeline protested.

"I just don't see how that's possible." Noah looked at the schedule.

"You should do the lecture in San Diego," Angeline suggested.

Noah took off his reading glasses to look at her. "Me?"

"Yes," she said.

"But I . . . I'm not really . . . I'm more of a behind-the scenes guy," Noah protested.

"Have you been training?" Angeline asked.

"Well, yes," Noah answered.

"And you have mastered your gift?"

"For the most part," he said, hesitating.

"And you plan on using this gift to help humanity?"

"Yes, someday, but . . ."

"Then this is the perfect opportunity for you to step center stage."

"My gift isn't really oratorical. And I'm certain they don't want me to sit on the stage in silence while I recalibrate their chakra systems," he replied, shifting in his seat.

"You mean to tell me that you traveled across time and space, overcome untold challenges, and now that you are here . . . you are going to let a little stage fright stop you from fulfilling your vow?" Angeline asked archly, raising an eyebrow.

Everyone laughed.

"I'm just not sure what I will talk about," he admitted, reluctantly.

"You could recite the Declaration of Independence, for all they would care. Your gift is the most unique among all of us. You have the ability to change the entire experience of their human life within minutes. They won't care what you say, once they feel the change," she said.

"I'll do it," he conceded. "Then I'll meet you in Dallas."

***

The bright lights warmed Angeline's skin, creating a pink blush on her cheeks. The stylist spiraled a golden curl around her finger, placing it purposefully behind Angeline's ear. Suna sat in the chair next to her, having her lipstick touched up. She looked like a porcelain doll from heaven, Her pale skin was powdered to perfection and a touch of translucent mauve blush shimmered on her cheeks. Toby leaned back in his chair, reading a magazine, and Leuters sat with his eyes closed, straight spine, focusing his breath into his lower abdomen.

Jeremy popped into the studio to check on them. "Is everyone ready?"

"Noah isn't here yet." Toby looked up from his magazine.

Jeremy checked his watch. "Have we heard from him?"

"He's twenty minutes out," Angeline replied, not moving her head for fear of disrupting the stylist.

"He'll be here in time," Suna assured him.

"Okay," Jeremy said, pulling a chair next to Angeline. "We are just going to go over the basics: who you are, what you have been up to for the past couple of years, and your mission. It'll be nice and easy," he promised. "Then we will film interviews with Noah, Suna, Leuters and Toby, followed by the event, for B-roll footage, but the focus of the program will be on your interview."

Noah rushed into the room, toting his laptop case over his shoulder. Suna looked up in surprise, "Noah! You made it!"

He leaned forward and kissed her cheek. "Sorry, I'm late."

Jeremy stood and shook his hand. "No problem, we have plenty of time. Let's get you in makeup." He motioned to the stylist and the makeup artist.

Noah settled in the chair and brushes of all shapes and sizes combed through his hair and buffed his cheeks.

"How was your debut?" Angeline asked.

"Thrilling." Noah smiled.

"Did you recite the Declaration of Independence?" Toby asked with a smirk.

Noah laughed. "In my own way."

"I'll bet you did," Suna said, patting the back of his hand.

CHAPTER THIRTY-NINE

"Angeline," Jeremy addressed her formally. The camera was rolling. "You have had quite a couple of years since we last met."

"Yes." She smiled, the stage lights glistening on her lip gloss.

"Can you tell us about it?"

"They've been my best years," she said.

"And why is that?"

"I have stepped into my authentic self."

"And who, exactly, is your authentic self?"

"God," she answered.

"Are you telling me that you are God?"

"Yes. But I don't have a corner on the market. We all are an aspect of God. Since I have realized this, everything has changed. I treat myself as if I were sacred."

She paused. "And others, as well, because they are, too."

"We have heard this type of message before, from other teachers," Jeremy said. "But many have a hard time understanding exactly what this means. Can you explain it for the novices, like me?" He raised an eyebrow.

"Let me ask you a question. If you walked outside today and everywhere that you went—the grocery store, your school, your job—you were noticed and treated as if you fundamentally mattered to every person that you met, how would you feel by the end of the day?"

"I would feel like I had a pretty good day," Jeremy laughed.

"How would you feel after a year?"

"Like I had a good life," he answered.

"Exactly. If everybody decided to relate to others in this way, this planet would be a pretty great place to live."

"You make it sound so simple."

"That's because it is."

"Then why haven't we reached this utopian world yet?"

"Because when you feel bad, it's difficult to change. In general, we spend our days being stressed out by each other. Our bodies feel heavy and tired, so we have less energy to contribute to making the person next to us feel good," Angeline explained.

"So your prescription would be to make yourself happy first?"

"My prescription is to become healthy first. Happiness will follow when you feel fundamentally vibrant."

"So eating right and exercise?"

"Health isn't only physical. Eating well, exercise, saying *no* to things that drain you and *yes* to things that make you happy, but most importantly, spending time alone to nurture and develop yourself, as if you were God creating a great human being."

"I can see why so many people have been inspired by you," he said. "But there are critics."

"Yes," she said, her voice dropping. "Surprisingly, my viewpoint, which seems obvious to me, is controversial to some, because I haven't tied the existence of God to one particular religion but rather to each individual human."

"Does the controversy bother you?"

"Of course it bothers me. My heart wishes for harmony, but they have the right to create the world as they wish, just as I do. So we can each go about our daily lives, living in the way that makes us happy. If it makes them happy to criticize me, that is their right. But I will not change the song in my soul because someone else doesn't like the melody."

CHAPTER FORTY

"I think that went well," Noah said, closing the car door after Angeline had safely tucked her legs in. He started the car and drove to the exit. The sound of a commotion drew everyone's attention outside as their rented SUV exited the stadium garage.

"What's going on?" Toby asked, looking out the window.

A crowd of a hundred people stood in the parking lot, holding signs and milling about. When the car drove past the parking gate, the group swarmed like angry hornets.

"Witch!" a woman holding a sign bearing a cross bellowed.

"Witch! Witch! Witch!" the crowd roared.

"What?" Angeline breathed. "What are they talking

about?" And then she saw it. The portrait of Mago, the picture that bore a great resemblance to her face, was held on a signpost, with the word *witch* scrawled in angry red paint across its surface.

"*Ho . . . ly shit*," Toby breathed, looking around the crowd in disbelief.

"What should we do?" Angeline asked.

"Talk to them," Suna said, rolling her window down.

"Not a good idea," Noah said, pressing the passenger window control on his console.

"Just drive," Leuters suggested in a deep voice. "Ignore."

Noah stepped lightly on the gas, moving the car forward despite the people.

"The hotel is only a few blocks away," Toby said.

When they pulled into the hotel, the same type of protest had gathered.

"Well, they are organized. I'll give them that," Toby whistled.

Noah pulled up to the valet, who opened Suna's car door. A roar filled the interior of the car. Noah quickly exited the car and jogged around to meet the attendant.

"Call security," he ordered.

Toby spoke urgently to Angeline. "Stick close to me."

"Cover." Leuters draped his brown hoodie over her

head, patting her shoulder reassuringly.

Angeline tried to control the tremble in her body. She was terrified.

"This is private property," the security guard yelled. "If you are not a guest here, you must leave!"

Toby opened the door, quickly guiding Angeline out of the car. Leuters followed.

"It's her!" someone yelled.

"Satan!" a man yelled, throwing an egg. It missed Angeline by inches.

Someone pushed Angeline roughly, knocking her to the ground. "Devil-infected daughter of Satan! Repent to the one Lord and Savior!"

Leuters stepped forward protectively. He shoved the man who had pushed her, sending him flying into the crowd. He helped Angeline to her feet and shielded her from the crowd with his massive body.

"You don't push a girl, you lunatic!" Toby hollered as he jumped into the crowd after the man and tackled him. Noah intervened, pulling Toby away while Leuters and Suna swept Angeline into the crowded lobby.

"They worship her!" a man holding a replica of the painting of Mago yelled. "Devil!"

Angeline cried, but not for herself. She loved them. Her heart overflowed with it. And they were so entrenched in fear that they threw eggs and called her the Devil.

Noah shouted at the front desk attendant, "Call the police, now!"

"I already have, Dr. Whitley." She was startled. "They're on their way."

Noah softened when he saw that he had upset her. "Please send the general manager to my suite, immediately."

"I will, Dr. Whitley," she said, picking up the phone and dialing.

CHAPTER FORTY-ONE

"This is harassment." Toby paced.

"It's their right to protest." Noah sat on the couch, stirring cream into his morning coffee.

"Can't we get them to go away?" Angeline asked.

"They have tried. The manager called the police, but the sidewalk is public property." Noah peeled a banana. "Eat something. Making yourself sick over it won't help. We've got to keep ourselves strong."

Angeline looked out the window and watched the angry crowd mill about. "We aren't dumping poison into the ocean, we aren't producing negative information, we aren't even forcing people to believe anything by threat of the sword," Angeline sighed. "But they treat us more severely than those who do."

Noah stepped behind her and placed his hand on

her shoulder. "Anytime a new concept is introduced into the mass consciousness, the old consciousness pushes back on it."

Angeline turned around. "It's barbaric."

"It's expected. Some will always resist anything that contradicts the model of the world they have been taught, because it threatens the very foundation that their lives have been built on. Think about how Galileo was laughed at when he suggested the Earth was not the center of the universe, or the civil war that was started after the idea was introduced that one man cannot own another man."

"People are crazy," she said.

"That's why we have come to help. We must make sure that we—"

Noah's thought was interrupted when Toby's cellphone dinged crazily, jumping and jingling as if it were possessed.

"What the . . . ?" Toby jumped to his feet when he examined the screen.

"What?" Leuters, who had been meditating with Suna on the other side of the room, opened his eyes. He had heard Toby's thoughts. Toby nodded his head in confirmation and sank into the couch without a word. He was in shock.

"What is it?" Noah sat upright, looking from Leuters to Toby. Neither one said a word. Noah stood and grabbed Toby's phone. It still buzzed with various vibrations, rings, and tones. He examined the screen.

"Suna," Noah said, beckoning to her.

"What's wrong?" Angeline asked, urgently.

"Toby's turn," Leuters breathed. "Is bad."

"Toby's turn for what?" Suna took the phone from Noah. She read the message on the screen aloud. "Toby, missing after a series of stock manipulations, federal warrant issued for his arrest, under investigation . . . Toby, is this true?"

"I'm not sure." Toby sat back.

"How can you not be sure?" Suna asked.

"I . . ." Toby was at a loss for words. "It could be. Sometimes I used my gift for . . . and I could have repeated something that I knew, but I never technically broke the law."

"Technically?" Suna asked.

"Everything was different back then," he stammered. "I wasn't in my right mind. I maneuvered around the laws but never broke them."

"Do you think that you could have been framed?"

"Maybe," Toby said. "Someone could have struck a deal with the U.S. Attorney's office to save their own skin. But whatever the case, this isn't good."

"What does this mean?" Suna asked.

"You'll have to go on without me," Toby answered.

"We have to keep our heads on straight," Noah said, calmly. "Mago warned us about this. We will be hit from every possible angle. The vow that we took transcends our pasts, even the system of the law." He turned to Leuters. "We must protect him from the system. The fate of the world depends on it."

Leuters nodded his head. "We keep him safe."

Noah turned to Toby. "Does anyone know that you are here?"

"I've used my credit cards," Toby admitted.

"We have to get you out of here," Noah said. "We can't fly commercial. Toby, do you know anyone in Texas with a private plane that we can borrow?"

"Yeah, there is a guy who owes me a favor." Donnie Anderson, of Donnie Oil, owed him a favor.

"Can you trust him?" Noah sat beside him.

"Yeah," Toby sighed. It seemed a shame to cash in his blank check for the use of a private plane. But they didn't have a choice. They had to get out of there fast. "Who will fly it?"

"Leuters," Noah answered.

"Where did you learn to fly?" Toby asked, surprised.

"Africa," Leuters replied.

"Where will we go?" Angeline asked. "They'll expect us to return to the BOS Resort."

"I know a place," Suna interjected.

"We have to move fast." Noah looked around the room. "Let's meet in the lobby in twenty minutes. Have your bags packed. Above all, keep a low profile."

There was a somber fog in the air; no one spoke.

***

Angeline rolled her luggage into the lobby and was stopped by a Federal Agent in a blue jacket that had *FBI* stamped in yellow. Her heart stopped. She searched the room for a sign of Toby.

"Excuse me, miss," he said, showing her his badge. "Are you a guest here?"

"I have a room here, yes," she confirmed, providing as little information as possible.

"Have you seen this man?" He flashed a picture. *Leuters.*

"I'm sorry, I can't help you." She smiled politely.

He handed her a business card. "If you do, call this number. He is an international fugitive."

Angeline nodded in acknowledgement and continued rolling her luggage through the lobby. Her heart beat uncontrollably, her nerves wracked to the point of lunacy. She saw no sign of Toby, Leuters, Noah or Suna.

"Where should I go?" she whispered under her breath. She had to get out of the lobby, filled with police officers, Interpol, and federal agents. But outside was no safe haven, either. A group of a hundred protestors gathered, all wanting to burn her at the stake. She looked around the room.

"Noah." She breathed a sigh of relief. "Where is everyone?"

"They're in the car," he answered quietly. "They're waiting in a parking lot down the street," he said, taking her elbow and leading her out the front door.

"They're here for Leuters." Angeline cast a glance to the agent who had stopped her.

"I know." He opened the door for her to exit. "Stick close to me," he murmured. "Just keep your eyes on the ground."

Noah led Angeline through the gauntlet of protestors.

"Witch!" one yelled.

"Criminals!" another bellowed.

"You will burn in hell! Blasphemer!"

"Accept the Savior into your heart and repent your sins!"

"Deny not the Lord and Savior; desist claiming

that you are God."

The crowd buzzed with a strange exuberance.

"If only they had such passion for ending war and feeding the hungry children of the world," Angeline said to Noah under her breath.

"Keep walking," he warned.

The crowd followed them as they walked down the street. Angeline focused on nothing but the next step ahead of her. Something hit her in the back of the head.

"Keep walking," Noah repeated.

Angeline felt the air around her ionize in an instant. Her awareness dimmed as Angeline pulled deep into her brainstem, allowing Mago to observe the world through her eyes. She begged Mago to let her continue to the car without incident. Mago didn't grant her request.

She turned around to face the crowd. Twenty people stared at her with the condemnation that could only be inspired by true desperation. Mago gave Angeline the choice: face her critics with scorn or love. Angeline felt compassion for them, sorry that a world existed that could twist the holiness so completely out of the soul.

"Love," she said aloud. At once, her heart opened and Mago's energy bloomed from within her. She felt her aura pulse with a spectacular white light—the repetition of its waves mimicking the vibration of a booming speaker. Angeline spoke, but it wasn't she who formed the thoughts.

"I have seen everything," she said, in an even but soft voice. "I was here before the Christ, and every teacher before and after. I am the spirit of the Earth. The love that I feel for you is evident in every flower that blooms, every forest that enables you to breathe. Yet you are so lacking in love that you invent imaginary gods that love you and hate others. The time for these mind games is running out. You must recover your true spirit or the planet is doomed. I cannot sustain your greed by my own blood for much longer. Please, open your heart and desist being ruled by invented systems of control and gain. Find your love, and I shall increase it a thousandfold, this I promise you."

The crowd stopped due to the sheer greatness of the energy that she emitted. It created a phenomenon that made it impossible to move their bodies without great effort, as if they were faced with a gale force wind. A few people, who had a predisposition enabling them to receive love, heard her and tears ran down their faces, awakened by the wordless illumination that she offered. Others were not present enough to be moved by the gift she had just given them. They pulled out their cell phones and recorded video footage. It was to those few that she now spoke.

"You say that I blaspheme because I have declared that God is within you, but it is you who blaspheme because you think that God is separate from you. If you do not change the information in your brain, the death of your world will be by your own hand," she said. "How many children have to cry before you feed them? How dark does the sky have to become before you stop pumping poison into it? How much money do you have to scavenge before you wake up and realize that it isn't real?"

As quickly as Mago's energy had descended, it lifted. Angeline blinked. The SUV screeched to a stop beside them.

Noah opened the door. "Get in!" he ordered.

Angeline slipped into the car. He closed the door behind her and jumped into the front seat.

"What was that all about?" Toby asked.

"Mago had something to say to them," Angeline replied, looking out the window at the crowd that she had just left. The once cohesive group seemed to be divided. She had left both tearful hugs and angry outbursts in her wake. Yet, it seemed that even the angry protestors looked upon their heart-softened counterparts with open curiosity, wondering what could have caused such a drastic and sudden change of heart.

"You remember?" Leuters asked. Previously, when Mago had spoken through Angeline, she had had no memory.

"Most of it, I think," she said. "It's a little fuzzy."

"So much for a low profile," Toby chuckled.

Suna stepped on the gas, accelerating. The airport was only a few minutes away, but they would have to move fast. The authorities were close behind.

CHAPTER FORTY-TWO

Alexandro rocked back on his heels. When he had turned on the television last night, he had no idea that he would find his brother, Leuters, giving an interview on *Dateline*, openly discussing MFS. Alexandro immediately called Interpol and alerted them of his brother's whereabouts. Leuters had not fulfilled the terms of his probation when he fled to another country. Alexandro caught a red-eye flight to Dallas in order to witness his brother being apprehended by the authorities, but somehow Leuters had eluded them.

While Alexandro waited in the lobby of the hotel, he noticed Noah and Angeline, two of the interviewees that partnered with Leuters for the live airing of last night's event. His heart surged with excitement. He followed them down the street, blending into a group of protesters. Not only did he get a picture of the license plate of the car that picked them up and sped off, but he got more evidence that would damn his brother.

He replayed the video of the blonde on his cell phone and laughed. It was perfect. Once again, Leuters, by association with this blonde woman who claimed to be the Mother of the Earth, had made a very powerful enemy. There were no institutions on the planet more powerful than the three religions. And they would not rest until Leuters and his little sacrilegious friends had paid for this most recent sin. He tucked his phone into his pocket and walked back to the hotel. This was a very good day.

CHAPTER FORTY-THREE

Leuters skillfully lifted off the runway, thanking his lucky stars that Toby had an acquaintance with a private passenger plane. One of the ground crew had received a radio call moments before their liftoff, threatening to delay their departure. Leuters held his breath, hoping that it wasn't the authorities on the other end of the line. He let out a sigh of relief when the technician nodded his head and waved his arm, indicating that they were cleared for liftoff. It seemed that the fates were finally in their favor.

"How long until we get there?" Noah asked. They were traveling to the small airport located at the Grand Canyon.

"Hour and half," Leuters replied, navigating through the sky.

"K'ete-t will pick us up when we land," Suna said. K'ete-t, her mentor, had raised her from the time she was a young girl, teaching her everything she knew. It was a very special relationship. The best part was that he lived off the grid, so tracking them would be next to impossible.

"Despite everything, I'm glad to have the chance to see where you grew up," Angeline offered.

"It's a very special place," Suna said.

"It must be." Angeline couldn't imagine the type of environment that had created this liberated human being. Suna was wise beyond her years and glowed with goodness and compassion. She didn't have a selfish bone in her body.

"K'ete-t can help us figure out what we should do next," she said.

"I don't even know *which way is up* anymore," Angeline breathed.

They flew in silence. Each person was lulled into a state of reflection. Angeline had been so drawn into thought, trying to work out their varied predicaments, that she wasn't sure how long they had been traveling when she heard the loud metal clank at the tail of the plane. The engine whined.

"What's wrong?" Angeline asked with alarm. The

plane bounced, causing Angeline to fall back into her seat.

"Put your lap belt on!" Noah ordered.

Angeline clicked the belt on with shaking fingers. The plane jumped again, and Leuters swore in Spanish, fighting to keep the craft steady in spite of the turbulence.

Leuters yelled, "Hold on!"

The plane rolled sideways. Angeline held tightly onto her seat and tried to control her nausea.

Leuters struggled to keep the plane airborne. The best he could do was guide the nose down for a water landing. The craft hovered above the river running through the floor of the Grand Canyon. He tried to set it down softly.

"Brace yourself!" Noah barked.

Another loud bang as one of the wings caught the branch of a tree and flipped, tearing it in two. The cabin was propelled forward and landed in the water, upside down. The impact was instant and jarring.

***

Noah took a breath before the cabin filled with water. He struggled to find his seatbelt and unbuckle it. His years as a surgeon had trained him to focus, keying into the moment to act without thought or emotion. His head broke the surface of the water. The deafening whir of the engine and screams filled his ears.

He saw Toby, treading water.

"Angeline!" Toby yelled. He dove into the water, returning a moment later.

"Where is she?" Noah yelled.

Toby shook his head.

"Leuters?" Noah called. "Suna?"

Toby looked around, dazed.

Noah dove underwater and swam back to the cabin. Suna's limp body was tethered to her chair by the safety harness. Noah quickly unbuckled it and swam with her to the shore. He checked her pulse. There was none.

He administered CPR, pumping her chest and breathing into her mouth several times. She coughed, vomiting water. She opened her eyes and blinked.

"Can you speak?" Noah asked urgently. "Suna, say something!"

"What happened?"

"We were in a plane crash."

"What?" Her voice rose with panic.

"Our plane crashed," Noah repeated.

Tears streamed down her temples. "Angeline?"

"Toby's looking for her," Noah said. "Can you move?"

"Maybe." She pushed herself weakly to her elbows.

Noah breathed a sigh of relief. "You're going to be fine. I have to find the others."

She nodded her head, pushing herself up further to try and help.

"Give yourself a minute," he said. "Reorient yourself, then come." He patted her shoulder and jumped to his feet.

Toby walked the shore, disoriented. He looked for Leuters and Angeline. He could hear Leuters scream, but couldn't find him.

"Where are they?" Noah hollered.

"I don't know!" Toby searched the tree line.

Another scream.

"Over here!" Toby yelled.

Noah jogged down the shore.

"Here!" Toby waved.

Leuters was trapped under a pile of debris. He screamed again.

"Hold on." Toby tried to be reassuring, "We've got you."

"You're going to be okay." Noah said.

"Are you hurt?" Toby asked.

Leuters took a second to assess his condition. "Shoulder pinned. And leg, prosthetic."

"Can you move your other leg?" Noah asked.

Leuters was quiet for a moment. "Toes wiggle."

"Good," Noah said. "Just give us a second."

Toby and Noah examined the wreckage. Sheets of metal were stacked in a multilayered and complex web.

"You lift that." Noah motioned to the metal pinning his shoulder. "And I'll free his leg." He turned to Leuters. "Buddy, on the count of three, I'm going to need you to scoot yourself out from under this."

Leuters nodded. Noah braced his shoulder under the steel and met Toby's eyes.

"One, two . . . three," he grunted, lifting the steel. Leuters's shoulder was released but the metal structure shifted and fell on top of Leuters's legs.

"Argh!" Leuters screamed.

Noah dropped the pole that he had shouldered.

"My leg!" Leuters howled.

Noah dove to the ground to look under the wreckage. Leuters's remaining leg was sliced straight through the bone. It hung by a network of arteries and nerves. Noah struggled to catch his breath. Leuters was losing blood fast.

"You are going to be okay," he said, trying to remain calm.

Leuters's face paled, and his lips turned blue.

His body shivered.

"Leuters, stay with me." Noah tapped his cheek.

Leuters turned his head, looked through fluttering lids. "Tell father, love him."

"You are going to be fine," Noah said. "Stay with me."

"Tell him . . . thank you," Leuters breathed.

"I'm going to fix this," Noah promised. He turned to Toby. "Come to this side. I'm gonna need you to lift while I pull him out."

Toby ran to the side of the wreckage where Noah stood. He braced the steel over his shoulders.

"Now!" Noah called.

Toby grunted as he stood, raising the metal.

"Hold it!" Noah called, weaving his wrists under Leuters's arm and pulling his body free of the wreckage. The few veins that connected his leg snapped.

"Argh!" Leuters yelled, grimacing. He passed out.

"Hold it!" Noah barked, crawling under the wreckage to retrieve Leuters's severed leg.

"I can't," Toby strained, grunting through gritted teeth.

"You're done," Noah said, once he had cleared the wreckage. The metal crashed to the ground, clanging like thunder. "Get Suna and find Angeline!" he ordered. He swept his belt off his waist and tightened it around

Leuters's thigh to stop the blood from flowing. "When you find her . . . get help!"

***

Suna stumbled up the shore as Toby desperately searched for Angeline.

"Where is she?" he asked.

Suna shook her head. They ran, weaving through the tree line, looking for her.

"Angeline!" Toby called.

"Angeline!" Suna yelled.

Toby found her first. She lay on the ground, dazed. Her eyes were open, slightly.

"I found her!" he called to Suna. "Over here!"

He wiped her hair from her brow. Her skin was clammy.

"Angeline." Tears welled in his eyes. "Angeline, you have to get up."

Her eyes shifted to meet his, but they didn't focus.

"Get up," he said more firmly. "You're okay. Get up."

Her breath was shallow.

"Toby?" she breathed.

"It's me," he cried.

She smiled and winced.

"Where does it hurt?" he asked.

"What happened?" she asked, confused.

"We were in an accident. You're going to be okay," he said.

Suna slid toward them from a run to a full stop. "How is she?" She knelt by Angeline's side.

"I don't know," Toby cried.

"Angeline?" Suna said. "Honey, I need you to try and get up."

"Suna?" Angeline smiled.

"Yes, sweetheart," Suna said. "Please, try and get up."

"I always thought you were so pretty," Angeline whispered.

"I need you to get up now. You are very important to this world."

"I'm tired," Angeline coughed. She closed her eyes and exhaled. She did not draw another breath in.

It took Toby a second to comprehend. He looked at Suna, then back to Angeline.

"Angeline!" Toby shook her roughly. "Angeline! Get up."

"Check her pulse," Suna ordered.

Toby released her shoulders. Suna pressed her fingers to her throat. She tilted her head and breathed into her mouth. "Pump her chest ten times."

Toby pumped. Suna checked her pulse. Once again,

she tilted her chin, and breathed into her mouth. "Pump!"

Toby pumped her chest with his palms, crying. They administered CPR for over twenty minutes.

Suna checked her pulse. "She's gone."

"No!" Toby protested. "Do it again!"

Suna placed her hand on Toby's shoulder and shook her head. She dropped her head into her hands and wept, her body racked with every sob.

"No," Toby cried. "Angeline." He slapped her cheeks. "Please, please," he begged. "I need you," he pleaded. "We need you. Please, don't be gone." He shook her again. "Angeline . . . Mago . . . No." The pain in his heart was just as deep as the pain he'd experienced as a young boy when his mother died, and again as a teenager when his Nana died. "Please don't leave me!" he begged.

CHAPTER FORTY-FOUR

"She's gone." Toby buried his face into her chest and wept. He couldn't feel her essence anymore. What animated her, *what made her*, was gone. It was just a body that he now held. He knew that. Yet, he couldn't put her down. He couldn't bring himself to let her go, not yet. "What are we going to do?" he wept, looking to Suna for answers.

"I'm not sure." She touched Toby's shoulder and tears flowed down her cheeks, dripping into the sand.

Toby felt like his heart was twenty miles deep, and every inch of that empty space filled with despair. "She was supposed to help us."

"We have to go on without her," Suna said.

"*Without her?*" Toby despaired. For too long, he'd trudged through the endless and complex systems of darkness within his mind and environment. Meeting her had granted him, for what turned out to be only moments, a reprieve. He had bathed in the sunlight of her goodness. He let it warm his soul and, for the first time in as long as he could remember, he felt hope. It was an incredible lightness of being that looked forward to a bright and expansive future. And now her sun would shine no longer, not for him, not for anyone.

"We have to go on," Suna repeated.

"Do we?" Toby asked. He looked at Angeline's face and remembered the light of enthusiasm that had shone from her eyes when she had defined happiness as *falling asleep being completely satisfied, excited that she got to wake up and do it all again.* But she wouldn't get to do anything again. She was dead. Gone. And she had taken both his heart and his hope with her when she left.

"We promised," Suna said. "We are the only ones who can help them remember." Suna rubbed his shoulder. "You have to pull yourself together."

"Help them remember," Toby whispered. "Of course." He would take Angeline's place. He would step forward and become the embodiment of Mago for the people of the Earth. Through him, she would live on.

"Toby," Suna warned. The way she said his name

sent shivers down his spine. He looked up. A mountain lion crept toward them, its body moving with cautious prowess.

Toby had never seen a mountain lion up close before. Its large muscular frame and wild eyes intimidated him. His body trembled uncontrollably.

"Hold absolutely still," Suna whispered.

The lion moved closer, very slowly. His eyes were fixed on Toby.

"I think he wants you to put her down," Suna said.

"No," Toby said quietly.

The lion snarled. Every nerve in Toby's body urged him to flee, but his heart wouldn't let him. He stared into the mountain lion's unforgiving gaze and silently implored the creature to leave them be.

"Toby, put her down."

Toby looked at Angeline. He couldn't, wouldn't let her go. His peripheral vision caught the movement of the lion as it crept closer. Toby leaned his body over hers protectively and squeezed his eyes shut. Even if this were to be his last moment, he wouldn't let her go. She was too precious to him to just leave her.

Another mountain lion appeared from the trees. It approached more quickly than the first lion and growled territorially. Toby felt their intent gaze like hot lasers boring into his nervous system, but he wouldn't be moved. He held absolutely still and begged them to leave with every thought in his mind.

A bald eagle swept down and landed near Angeline's shoulder. It fanned its massive wings and squawked.

When Toby saw the eagle, he understood. The mountain lions hadn't come to eat her, they had come as companions to his mourning. They were no longer something to be feared, nor were they separate from him. They had joined together with one mind.

Two rattlesnakes with thick bodies slithered and coiled themselves around her ankles. From every direction, animals appeared: black bears, elk with their majestic antlers, bobcats, fox, deer, squirrels, mice, and beavers. A flock of birds descended from the sky, every bird imaginable, all coming to gather around her body. Toby set Angeline down and backed away so that the animals might have their moment to bid her goodbye.

"How is this happening?" Toby asked.

Suna opened her sixth chakra and looked at the world before them. A majestic aquamarine cloud with swirls of light, like little sparkling strings of silver and gold that weaved to and fro, billowed from the Earth. The energy that rose around Angeline's body took form. It was her oversoul, Mother Mago.

Suna grabbed Toby's hand so that he could connect to her spiritual sight.

"I see it," he breathed.

The animals lowered their heads, yielding in reverence. Mother Mago's voice echoed through the land, though her lips did not appear to move.

"The time for your journey to end is not now, Angeline. You have a mission to fulfill." She swept her palm over Angeline's body in a figure eight, starting with her forehead, crossing over the heart, and ending at the lower abdomen. The motion of her hand created two vortexes; energy poured into her forehead and shone out of her abdomen, filling the space around them with twinkling particles of life. Angeline's body took a breath.

"She's alive," Toby breathed, moving toward her.

Suna stopped him before he stepped into the realm of the aquamarine clouds. "Toby, wait," she warned, pulling his hand.

The grass and ivy under Angeline's body grew impossibly fast, creating a natural mattress beneath her body that was fit for a princess. Flowers burst into bloom all around them in an instant, releasing an otherworldly scent that was so aromatic that Toby could taste it on his tongue. This was the fragrance of

Mother Mago's soul.

As suddenly as the natural phenomenon had started, it stopped. Like a channel being changed on a television set, one minute Toby was watching Mother Mago perform a miracle and the next moment everything was normal. The air was clear and the animals that had gathered dispersed. Angeline opened her eyes and stretched, as if waking from nothing more than a peaceful slumber.

"You're alive!" Toby shook off Suna's hand and rushed to embrace her. He buried his face in her hair, which was infused with the magical scent of Mago's soul.

"Of course I'm alive," she said.

Toby pulled back. "You don't remember what happened?"

Angeline looked around, confused. "Did we land?"

Suna knelt beside them, touching Angeline's face with her palm. "You are a miracle. Because of you I believe."

"Believe what?" Angeline asked.

"That we will achieve what we came here to do."

"You came back," Toby breathed. "It has to mean something."

"Came back?" Angeline asked.

"You were dead," Suna said, tucking a strand of hair

behind Angeline's ear. "But you came back. We have been granted a very powerful sign."

CHAPTER FORTY-FIVE

Noah looked up as they approached. "Did you get help?" He crouched near the unconscious Leuters, tending to his wounds. He had created a makeshift bandage around Leuters's thigh with his shirt and had used his pants to wrap Leuters's severed leg. "I don't know how much longer he has," he said. "He lost a lot of blood and his pulse is weak."

"We can help," Suna said, rushing to Noah's side. "Angeline?"

"I don't know what to do. His leg is . . . ." She looked at the bloody bundle and didn't even want to utter the word.

Gone. His leg is gone.

Suna touched her shoulder. "Angeline, you need to focus. Now is the time for you to challenge your limits.

You'll know what to do."

Angeline knelt by Leuters's side and closed her eyes. She had performed some pretty miraculous feats in her life, but this was so much bigger. She prayed to Mother Mago for help and was relieved when she heard an immediate response echo within her.

I am the law. I am the way that nature works, the providence. I am what quantum physicists encounter when they go into the atomic world—and you are my emissary. Whatever I can do, you can do too.

Angeline's body trembled with power. She opened her eyes and picked up Leuters's leg. "Please wash this in the river."

Toby grabbed the leg and ran to the water. "I'll be right back."

Angeline turned to Noah. "When he returns, remove the bandage and hold the leg in its proper place," she instructed. "Please be very quiet and keep your thoughts neutral."

"I understand," Noah said, removing the bandage.

"Suna, I need your help too."

"Anything." Suna knelt beside her.

"Take his head into your hands and focus your energy through his circulatory system."

"I will," Suna promised, moving to kneel above his

body. She held his head in her palms.

"I will begin now. Please don't interrupt me." Angeline closed her eyes.

Toby returned with the leg. "I have it!"

"Shhhh," Suna quieted him.

Toby passed the leg to Noah, who placed it exactly as Angeline had instructed. He pressed the two ends together firmly. Noah had been present for countless surgeries. He himself, on many occasions had, as it is often said, played God. In his wildest dreams, he'd never anticipated a situation like this.

Toby watched as the three focused their attention on healing Leuters's body. Angeline held her palms over the wound. There was nothing supernatural about what he saw. No thunderbolts, no lightning, just an accelerated process of healing.

Once the leg was fully healed, without even a scar, Angeline moved her hands to his chest. "He will need water when he wakes," she said, though her eyes remained closed.

He'd lost a lot of blood. Once again Toby ran to the stream, this time in search of water.

Angeline shook his body, gently. "Leuters, open your eyes."

He blinked and sprung up in alarm. "My leg!" he

cried, looking down to discover nothing was amiss. "I dream it gone," he wept, running his hands along its surface as if it were the most precious treasure in the world.

"It wasn't a dream," Noah said.

Leuters looked up. He didn't understand. He wiggled his toes. "I dream plane crash and my leg got cut," he said, looking around. He spotted the wreckage.

"It happened," Suna said, kneeling beside him.

Toby brought water from the stream that he had collected with his shoe. He handed it to Leuters. "Sorry, it was the best I could do."

Leuters gulped it thankfully. When he was finished, he returned the shoe to Toby. "More?" he asked.

"You got it, buddy." Toby sprung to his feet, running to the water once more.

Leuters looked at his leg. "How?"

Both Suna and Noah looked at Angeline.

"Angeline do this?" Leuters asked.

"Your body did this." Angeline smiled. "I just made it a little faster. But your prosthesis was crushed in the accident," she said. "Mago wanted me to tell you that she has sent us assistance." She raised her chin to the tree line. A moment later, three mules emerged from the forest.

CHAPTER FORTY-SIX

The walk was long and arduous, but their hearts had been strengthened by both faith and hope. They weren't alone in their quest; the recent miracles had proven that.

The three mules were ridden by Angeline, Suna and Leuters. Toby and Noah walked beside them on foot. They ate what food they could scrounge, drank what little water they could find. It had been a four-day journey, but they were close to their destination.

Suna had explored these canyons as a girl, and she knew them well. Her teenage years had been spent in a nearby off-grid community created by her mentor.

"How did you meet K'ete-t?" Angeline asked.

"When I was fifteen, both of my parents died. It was a difficult time in South Korea; we were a third-world country."

"Did you meet him in Korea?" Noah asked.

"No," she said. "I had a distant cousin in America. After my parents died, she offered to bring me here to provide me with the opportunity for a greater education. But when I got here, instead of sending me to school, as she had promised, she sent me to work as a seamstress. The hours were long, and the conditions were," she paused to consider, "intense," she finished. Her voice dropped. "She collected my pay every week and told me that I had to earn my keep, which was a small room in her house, no bigger than a closet. I'd never met her before coming to America, and soon discovered that she wasn't a very noble person."

Angeline hummed sympathetically.

"It wasn't all bad," Suna said. "In many ways, she granted me the ultimate gift, which was meeting K'ete-t. When I met him, everything changed."

"Meeting destined," Leuters huffed. "Two souls take any road, endure much hardship, to get together as quick as possible."

"Yeah." Suna smiled. "Meeting him was such a homecoming that it was easy to let go of the pain of my past."

"What happened next?" Toby asked.

"After two years of working in the glorified sweat

shop, I put my shoes on one morning and headed to work, but something inside wouldn't let me open the door to the factory," Suna said. "I walked the town all day, knowing that if I returned home, having not gone to work, I would be badly beaten. It was the late seventies, and hitchhiking was quite popular. So I stuck out my thumb and let fate decide where I would land. Fate, as it turned out, would put me into K'ete-t's passenger seat. Meeting him was a revelation. He brimmed with such enthusiasm, such hope for the world. I had never heard anyone talk about humanity in the way that he did. I never considered that things could be better, but listening to him opened new horizons in my heart. He made the impossible seem possible. We became fast friends, and he invited me to become a student at his school."

"What type of school was it?" Toby asked.

"I think rather than explaining it, I should perhaps let you experience for yourself. Let's just say that I could have never imagined something so . . . well, life affirming."

"And this is where we're going now?" Toby said, holding the mane of the donkey to keep pace as he walked beside her.

"Yes," Suna said. "I am excited for all of you to

meet him."

"What's he like?" Toby asked.

Suna considered. "True," she answered in one word.

"You're not going to give me more?" Toby raised an eyebrow.

"I suppose each person experiences him differently because he's a clear mirror."

"What does that mean?" Toby asked, remembering the tiny bronze mirror in his pocket.

"In him, you see your own nature, favorable or not. He reflects the truth, whatever it may be."

"I'm confused," Toby said.

"Some people describe him as a grandfather, some as a teddy bear, some as an enlightened master, some as a tree-hugging hippie," Suna laughed. "But he is none of those things. Those are just labels. He simply holds space and reflects what's in front of him, so that the person may witness themselves without filter and grow from that experience. Because of this, people have a varied reaction to him. Some love him intensely; some hate him intensely. But it is only the reflection of themselves that they love or hate."

"What does he reflect to you?" Toby furrowed his brow, trying to grasp the nature of her mentor.

"I find him to be the most considerate, selfless human being on the planet. And not because that is my nature reflected back, but because I have witnessed years of him reflecting the truth, no matter how unpopular it may be. In every moment he gives himself up, letting go of his ego, in order to help people grow. He is not fixed. He moves through each and every moment with fluidity and truth. He is a *Seuseungnim*."

"What's a *Seuseungnim*?"

"It means a guide."

"Guide to what?"

"A guide out of the illusion." Suna smiled. "Those little stories that wrap around us and keep us from expressing our true spirit. The more tightly you are wrapped in your illusion, the stronger he has to pull. But he doesn't force this awareness on anyone. He just holds space, creating the perfect conditions for the recognition of what is and the growth into what can be."

Suna stopped her mule. Turning around to address the group, she said, "This is the entrance of the canyon. It will be difficult to take the mules. I am afraid that we'll need to take the remaining terrain on foot."

"But Leuters . . ." Noah said.

"I'll help him," Toby offered. He stepped to Leuters's side, assisting him as he slid off the mule onto his remaining leg. Leuters patted Toby on the back.

He was grateful.

"I'll help too," Noah said. "Let me know if you get tired."

"I will, brother," Toby replied.

Suna and Angeline dismounted from their mules. Suna took a moment to walk from mule to mule, thanking them by holding her forehead against theirs and kissing their nose. She patted each on the backside and sent them into the forest.

Leuters leaned his weight on Toby's shoulders, and they hobbled down the rocky terrain. Toby was a changed man. He had completely abandoned his ego and bloomed into the noble warrior that he was born to be. The hard experiences of his life had been forgotten, his sins forgiven. Not by an external savior, but by his own soul. He felt like he had been reborn, become the person that he would have been if life hadn't gotten in the way. He had touched his true nature and felt like the hero that he always wished to be.

They walked the steep trail. Suna was in the lead, followed by Angeline, then Toby and Leuters, with Noah bringing up the rear. Their bodies moved without thought; only their physical energy carried them now.

When they rounded the last corner in the dark, they saw an iron-gated entrance with a little sign illuminated by a solar bulb that read, *Earth Citizen School.*

Suna almost cried with relief.

At long last, she was home.

CHAPTER FORTY-SEVEN

Suna wasn't sure how long she had slept. It could have been four hours or twelve. She couldn't remember a time when sleep had drawn her in so deeply. She stretched her arms and yawned, feeling the soft sheets from her youth caress her skin. Her room smelled the same. Like the desert, like water, like heaven. She rolled over and resisted the urge to fall back asleep. They'd had a tumultuous journey since leaving Sedona, and she was tired.

She slipped her slippers and housecoat on, tying the sash as she shuffled into the kitchen. She filled the teapot under the tap and heard a voice that made her heart glow.

"Suna," K'ete-t said.

He had taught her to love with the heart of heaven

and the might of the sun. No matter how much she matured, how versed in the world she became, how much
mastery over her thoughts and emotions she developed,
K'ete-t was the exception. She couldn't control the
emotion that rose within her, the sheer joy that overwhelmed her when she turned around and saw his face.

"Seuseungnim!" She dropped the tea kettle into the
sink and folded herself into his arms. The incredible
challenges she had endured were forgotten, and her
soul rested in a way that it only did when she was with
her mentor. His skin smelled the same, floral, and held
the same plumpness of an infant that it always had.
No matter how many years passed, how white his hair
became, his native face remained luminous. Nothing
makes the skin glow quite like the light of God.

He patted her hair. "I was worried about you."

"I know, Seuseungnim. I'm sorry, we have faced
many troubles since we last spoke."

"You are here now," he shushed reassuringly.

"At last," she breathed. "I have missed you."

"I'm always with you," he assured her.

"It's not the same," she said.

He laughed. She could practically hear the twinkle
in his eye.

She pulled out of the embrace, wiped the tears from

her cheeks and pressed her hand to her heart. It was warm with gratitude. "I have much to tell you."

He held her hand and led her to sit at the small table in the dining room.

"I find myself in a lot of trouble," she confided. "It's bad."

"Tell me about it," he said, furrowing his brow.

"The others and I joined together at Bell Rock and activated the vow. Ever since that moment, we have been wrapped in controversy and opposition. Our reputations are ruined, the BOS Resort is under attack, two of my associates are under investigation and law enforcement is looking for us. The church, the press, disaster, every trial imaginable has come at us from all directions, each one more despairing and urgent than the last. We haven't had a moment of peace nor have we been immune from any tragedy. We can't even catch our breath before the next catastrophe strikes. And our vow, which should be joyous, weighs heavily on my heart because I'm tired, Seuseungnim. Time is running out, and I'm not sure that we will make it against such odds. It's too much," she said, revealing her despair to her teacher.

He put his hand on her shoulder. "Breathe, my little Suna."

She took a shaky breath and exhaled. Her breath scarcely reached the top of her lungs. She had remained stoic through all of the tribulations. She had braced for the storm, but now, in the presence of such warmth, she could relax enough to realize how much damage had been done to her spirit in the process. What people fail to realize about enlightened beings is that they are sensitive. They feel tragedy deeper than most, though they may seem unwavering because of their strength.

K'ete-t considered all that she had shared. "You can handle whatever may come your way," he said, smiling. "Remember your ancestry; you have strength in your blood."

"I know," she exhaled, slumping her shoulders. "Sedona used to feel like my home but now . . . ." She shook her head. "It feels like the place where I will die."

"You must not be afraid of death, little Suna," he said. "I tell you again that death doesn't exist. It's an illusion."

"So is all of this," she laughed, indicating the world around them. "I know that everything is an illusion. But it doesn't make it any easier."

"Illusions are mutable, changeable. You have the power to change the entire dream for all of humanity. Imagine it, Suna," he encouraged. "Imagine the moment when your little soul that has traveled so far, endured so much, gets to witness every single human on the planet remember the heaven that exists within them. The trouble that you face pales in comparison to the glory that we are to witness. It's our destiny, and we have no choice but to complete it."

In her memory, she was transported back to the day that she met K'ete-t, when she had buckled her seatbelt and he shared his vision for a healthy humanity. His enthusiasm had been infectious then, just as it was now.

"You are right," she conceded. "The universe has supported us with many miracles. I do have hope, Seuseungnim. But I'm still tired."

"You have a full five minutes to either rest, cry, or complain. You can choose the way that you wish to release the stagnant emotions that heavy your heart. But after that, you must recover your spirit," he said, rising from his seat and patting her shoulder. "Your time starts now."

She laughed, giving in to his easy mood. She rose from her seat. "I think that what I need the most right now is a cup of tea with my Seuseungnim."

CHAPTER FORTY-EIGHT

"Oh, hello, little one." Angeline smiled at the nine-year-old girl with red hair and freckles who sat at the edge of the lake in half-lotus, pounding her abdomen rhythmically, as Angeline had done many times before. "What's your name?"

"Katrina," she said, smiling. Her body shook with every tap.

"And what are you doing, Katrina?" Angeline knelt to sit next to the young girl.

"My morning training," she answered.

Angeline watched the sun peek over the lake's horizon. "Do you wake up this early every morning?"

"Yes," Katrina answered. Something about this little girl was settled, wise beyond her years. She wore a white jersey tracksuit and sat upon a purple yoga mat, neatly placed on the shore. She looked like a little angel-in-training.

"I also like to get up early," Angeline said encouragingly, watching her. "Can you show me what you are doing?"

Katrina slowed the rhythm of her taps, demonstrating that she tapped the point two inches below her belly button.

"Am I doing this right?" Angeline tapped her abdomen in sync.

Katrina cast a glance to her side. "Yes. Tap a little more firmly," she suggested, sounding more like a professional than a girl.

"Why are we doing this?" Angeline asked.

"This is where our second chakra is," Katrina answered.

"And tapping helps our second chakra?"

"It wakes the vibration up," Katrina said. "Like jump-starting a car battery."

"Thank you for explaining," Angeline said. The two tapped in silence. Angeline loved the sensation of warmth that radiated through her abdomen. It was quite delicious. Her lungs relaxed, and her breath dropped. The sound of the rhythm lulled her mind into a comfortable and tranquil state. She opened her eyes—which, she realized, she had instinctually closed. "How long do we do this?" she asked.

"Until we stop thinking," Katrina answered.

Angeline laughed. "Is thinking bad?"

"No, thinking is good, but not having awareness or control over it isn't."

"Okay," Angeline chuckled. "We'll keep tapping."

Angeline felt a kinship with this little girl. She felt the overwhelming compulsion to pull Katrina into her arms and cuddle her, as a mother would. She wanted to protect her, love her and teach her everything that she could ever hope to know about life. Instead, she quietly basked in her love for this perfect little human being with red hair and a crooked smile.

The pitter-patter to her side lulled to a full stop. Angeline followed suit, resting her palms on her knees. She listened to the sound of her breath, felt the miracle of the exact moment that the air was absorbed into her lungs. She felt every beautiful sensation inside of this body and wondered why humans could never seem to find happiness. This body was positively filled with satisfying sensations. It was quite intoxicating, actually.

Katrina began to recite the ChunBuKyung. Angeline joined her.

"*Il. Shi. Mu. Shi. Il. Suk. Sahm. Geuk. Mu. Jin. Bohn.*

Chun. Il. Il. Ji. Il. Yi. In. Il. Sahm.
Il. Juk. Ship. Guh. Mu. Gwe. Hwa. Sahm.
Chun. Yi. Sahm. Ji. Yi. Sahm. In. Yi. Sahm.
Dae. Sahm. Hap. Yook. Saeng. Chil. Pahl. Gu. Woon.
Sahm. Sah. Sung. Hwan. Oh. Chil. Il.
Myo. Yun. Mahn. Wang. Mahn. Rhae.
Yong. Byun. Bu. Dong. Bohn.
Bohn. Shim. Bohn. Tae. Yahng. Ahng. Myung.
In. Joong. Chun. Ji. Il. Il. Jong. Mu. Jong. Il."

Chills ran along Angeline's skin as the energy she had generated in her abdomen shot up her spine, like mercury rising up a thermometer, and burst into her brain, like the explosion generated in the cosmos when the universe was created. She started laughing; she didn't know why. The sensations were a revelation.

Katrina cast an exasperated sideways glance, a clear indication that she didn't appreciate the disruption to her morning training.

"Sorry," Angeline apologized. This little girl was hilarious.

Katrina let out a long sigh. "That's okay. I'm just about done anyway."

"What else do you like to do?" Angeline asked.

"Play," Katrina answered.

"What do you play?"

"I can show you," Katrina offered.

"Oh, yes. Please do," Angeline breathed.

Katrina located a little ant crawling on the ground near her yoga mat. She watched the insect intently. Angeline could sense that the ant was being directed by the power of Katrina's mind. It traveled in little clockwise circles.

"That's amazing, Katrina." Angeline clapped her hands. "Why don't you try that with me? Think of anything that you want me to do. I will focus really hard and try to pick up what you are thinking, and you can tell me if I got it right."

"Okay," Katrina said, shifting her body toward Angeline. She focused intently.

Angeline laughed and scrunched her nose.

Katrina nodded her head emphatically.

"Try another one," Angeline suggested. Her cheeks tingled. She puffed them out like a puffer fish.

Katrina laughed, delighted by this game.

"Did I get it?" Angeline asked.

"Yes!" Katrina's excitement elevated another degree.

Angeline patted her belly three times then rubbed her palm in three circles. "How about now?"

Katrina nodded her head.

"Try another one," Angeline said.

Katrina concentrated really hard, trying to stump her. Angeline leaned forward and tickled Katrina's ribs with pinching fingers. "Did I get it?"

Katrina laughed and jerked her body away. "No!" she squealed.

"Are you sure?" Angeline teased, tickling her.

"Yes!" Katrina hollered through her laughter.

"I don't know . . . I think that this is what you told me to do. I just can't seem to control my fingers, they just keep moving," Angeline teased.

She tickled the girl until her cheeks bloomed roses and her eyes sparkled.

"Would you like to see me try?" Angeline asked.

Katrina nodded.

"Watch this," Angeline said, showing off. She closed her eyes and prayed to Mother Mago. A bird swooped from the sky and landed on her hand. Katrina's eyes widened with awe.

"Why don't you try?" Angeline suggested.

The little girl held out her hand. The bird hopped from Angeline's hand to hers, cooing and bobbing its head in a mating dance.

"I think he likes you," Angeline chuckled.

"I love him," Katrina breathed.

Three bells chimed in the distance, and the bird

flew from her hand.

"What was that?" Angeline asked.

"It's time to eat," Katrina said, gathering her yoga mat.

"Can I sit with you and your friends at breakfast?"

The little girl nodded. "Yes."

CHAPTER FORTY-NINE

Noah laid the last wrap of tape and admired his handiwork. Pitching the supplies he had scrounged from the garage the previous evening into the basket beside the work desk, he wrapped the project he had been working on in brown paper packaging and walked down the long hallway. He knocked on the door at the end of the hall.

"Come in," Leuters called.

Noah opened the door. "I have a present for you, *amigo*," he said, stepping into the room. He placed the package on Leuters's lap.

"For me?" Leuters quickly tore the paper. He examined the item. It took him a full minute to comprehend.

"I fixed it," Noah said, proudly.

Leuters held his prosthesis on his lap. It was wrapped in silver duct tape and looked like something you would find in a trash heap at the local dump.

"It's beautiful." Leuters was moved.

"Try it on," Noah encouraged.

Leuters slipped the plastic shell wrapped in silver tape over his leg and stood.

"Is it comfortable?" Noah asked. "It's not too tight, is it?"

Leuters walked about the room, stopped in front of Noah and opened his arms, pulling him into a bear hug. "Thank you," he said, squeezing tightly.

"You're fully mobile again," Noah said, overwhelmed to the point of tears by Leuters's gratitude. "You've been through too much in this lifetime, brother. I'm just sorry that I couldn't help more."

CHAPTER FIFTY

There was something incredible about this moment. Toby walked down the sand path of the garden, trying to identify what it was. This was a very ordinary morning, in an ordinary garden. The birds flitted from tree to tree in an ordinary way. What was extraordinary was *how* he witnessed the moment. He was fully present, maybe for the first time in his life. As it turned out, *presence* was the wonder drug he had been searching for his whole life. He had looked for this exact sensation at the bottom of whiskey bottles, down gold mines, and in the arms of many women. But nothing even came close.

He laughed. *What I was searching for was within me all along.* The problem was, he didn't know how he stumbled upon this presence of mind, and was uncertain if he would be able to replicate it at a later date. Perhaps it was the environment in which he found himself.

He stopped in front of a stone plaque at the entrance of the gated garden. *Earth Citizen School*, it read. He contemplated the meaning of the phrase. *What, exactly, is an Earth Citizen?*

A group of children, ranging from five to fifteen, sat at a table under a tree. They held tablets, touching the screens with quick fingers, as if they were in a contest to see who could tap the fastest. The most proficient, and perhaps the cutest, was an African American boy with a big forehead and black plastic-rimmed glasses. He couldn't have been more than seven years old, but he possessed an unusual confidence. Toby could have sworn that he was looking at the seven-year-old version of Noah, the future heart surgeon.

Another group performed a martial art on the lakeshore. It looked like Tai Chi, but with stronger movements. They were older, well-muscled boys and girls who wielded swords that sliced through the air as their bodies glided with acrobatic precision.

Everywhere Toby looked, there was a harmonious gathering of varied activities. There was order, and yet the children moved organically, as if they were free to do anything they chose, and what they chose was to move together as one. The children spoke to each other telepathically, which exceeded Toby's gift of reading minds. They mostly spoke about taking care of the bird of their soul, and communed with the flowers and animals as if they were sentient beings. Suna's other-worldly demeanor made sense. Having been reared in this environment, she moved through the often chaotic world as if she had never left. *You can take the girl out of the Earth Citizen School, but you can't take the Earth Citizen out of the girl.* He laughed.

He saw a teenage boy who seemed to be in a rush. The boy had unkempt dishwater curls. He held his tablet under his arm and stepped quickly, which looked out of place in this serene environment. Toby was intrigued. He followed him.

Toby walked lightly, attempting not to break any brush under the weight of his feet as he followed the boy into the forest. The boy stopped in a clearing, retrieved a picnic pad from a wooden box hidden under a low-hanging tree and laid it on the ground. He tapped the screen of his tablet and a slow and melodic symphony filled the forest, accompanied by the song of the birds. Toby knew where this was going. He, himself, had played this scene out many times when he was a teenager.

As if on cue, a girl with long dark locks and porcelain skin emerged from the trees. Her lips were plumped and looked like she had been eating cherries. She was a beautiful teenager who, he would bet, would mature into a classic beauty.

"Hi," she said timidly to the boy.

"Hi," he beamed. "Are you ready?"

She nodded her head, biting her lip. The young boy rushed forward and took her hands reassuringly. Toby resolved to give them their privacy, but something kept his feet from moving. His heart was moved, feeling as if he were witnessing the fruition of the slowest, sweetest, love story of all time. They were so innocent, cheeks blushing with ripe anticipation.

"Lie down here," he said, motioning to the blanket. He held her hands as she sunk to the blanket. He touched her cheek lightly and looked into her eyes. "We'll take this slow," he assured her. She nodded her head and closed her eyes.

He moved to sit next to her side, rested one palm on her abdomen, the other on her chest. Toby leaned forward. The placement of his hands was not erotic, as he had anticipated, but holy.

"Spirit of the Earth," the boy said quietly. "I ask to draw upon your energy. Callie's body needs to be filled with your restorative energies."

Tears fell down the side of Callie's face. She breathed deeply, as if pulling in every particle of life from the ether.

"If she truly is a child of the Earth, and we truly are children of heaven, as we have been taught, I beg for your help," he prayed. "Please, help her."

It was as if Toby were watching a scene of a younger version of himself and Angeline in the forest after the crash. Toby cried. This young girl with the timid smile and cherry-stained lips was sick. The boy hadn't called her to the forest to experience her body; he had called her here to heal it because he loved her.

Toby sunk to his knees and joined the prayer. Though he had never met her, he desperately wanted her to live. He resolved himself to introduce the two to Angeline, who would easily be able to help the girl.

CHAPTER FIFTY-ONE

At once, Angeline was surrounded by a buzz of joyful chattering children, just as if she was the little old lady who lived in the shoe. They practically climbed over each other to get her attention. She smiled, touching each child with light fingers, brushing stray hairs from sweaty brows, patting heads to reassure each glittering soul that they were both noticed and notable to her. She was careful to not leave a single one untouched by her love.

"Why don't we sit?" Angeline suggested.

"I get to sit next to you," Katrina breathed, gleaming with pride for having brought Angeline to the dining hall for all of her friends to take in until they were plump with love.

"Me, too!" a fair-skinned Korean girl called, weaving

her fingers through Angeline's.

"I want a turn," the African American boy with plastic-rimmed glasses whined.

"Can I?" another child hollered. "Me, too! Can I? Can I? Can I?" A chorus of prepubescent voices shrilled in symphony.

"Why don't I sit in the middle? That way everyone can sit around me," Angeline offered.

"You're going to sit in the middle of the table?" Katrina eyed the top of the rectangular table, concern marking her brow. She was certain that was against the rules.

Angeline giggled, patting Katrina on the head. "I will sit in a chair, like the rest of you. I'll just sit at the center of the table," she said, pulling out a chair. "Here . . ."

Twenty kids rushed to claim their seats, shuffling around in a frenzied game of musical chairs. The boy with black-framed glasses wasn't as fast as the others. He got the seat at the far end. He sat down and placed his elbows on the table, resting his cheek on his palm in the cutest gesture of dejection.

"What's your name, dear?" Angeline turned her attention to him, attempting to ease his tender feelings from any sense of isolation.

"Anthony," he said, perking up.

All of the children leaned forward in their chairs, attention rapt.

"Isn't this nice?" Angeline said, stretching her arms on the tabletop. "I'm enjoying my time with you very much. Thank you for inviting me to sit with you."

"I think you're pretty," the Korean girl confessed, blushing.

"Well, I think that you are quite pretty too."

"I like your hair," another girl piped in. "It's so shiny."

"And I think your soul is so shiny," Angeline countered, looking around the table. "You all give me such hope. Do you know what hope is?"

"That things will work out?" a boy with loose black curls and dimples answered.

"Yes, you make me feel that things will really work out," Angeline answered. "The world has been waiting for you for a very long time, and I am going to make sure that it is the best possible world for you to live in."

"We're gonna help too," Anthony said from the end of the table.

"I'll count on it," Angeline said. "How do you want to help? What is your dream?"

"My dream is to become the president of the United States," he answered, sitting up straight in his chair.

"I want to become a vegetarian," a five-year-old boy

with sun-kissed golden hair said. "I love animals," he declared proudly.

"Vegetarians do love animals," Angeline replied, repressing a smirk.

"Not vegetarian," Katrina corrected astutely. "Veterinarian." She emphasized the word syllable by syllable.

"Then what's a vegetarian?" he asked.

"A vegetarian is a person who only eats vegetables, nuts, and fruits," Angeline answered.

"You're making me hungry," another boy whined.

"I am also quite hungry," Angeline said. "Do they bring our meals to the table?" she asked, looking around the dining room.

"We're supposed to get our food there." Katrina pointed to a buffet-style table with both hot and cold foods.

"Well then, we should get our meals," Angeline said, looking around the table. The children watched her, unmoving. Understanding crossed her features. "How about this? I will watch your seats while you get your meals."

The kids looked around the busy cafeteria, assessing if they could trust that their seat would be reserved until they returned with their plate.

"Go on, I'll make sure that no one takes your seats," she promised.

CHAPTER FIFTY-TWO

Suna and K'ete-t walked the property to the main house. "Jiso has also returned to the Earth," Suna said. "It may not be a coincidence. There's a chance that his soul is playing out a vendetta."

K'ete-t stopped in his tracks. "Does he know who he is?"

"No," she answered. "He thinks that he is angry with his brother. He doesn't know how deep his hatred runs."

"You do not need to concern yourself with him," K'ete-t advised. "His soul has come for redemption. Simply being on the Earth during the transition of the eras will resolve his soul of its weight. He's very fortunate to have returned at this time."

They arrived at the main house. He opened the door and led Suna into his office, which was more of a meditation room. The octagonal room was painted in lavender with shelves lining the walls where crystals of all shapes and sizes glimmered in the light. At the center of the room was a drum, with a seating arrangement of multi-colored pillows placed around it. Angeline, Noah, Toby and Leuters waited for them, examining the portraits that hung on the wall. Everyone turned when they walked into the room.

"Hello," K'ete-t said. He seemed to glow with an otherworldly countenance.

"This is my mentor, K'ete-t," Suna said, introducing him.

"Please, let's sit." K'ete-t motioned to the pillows around the drum.

Noah was surprised to discover that there wasn't an air of pretension about K'ete-t. He wasn't sure what he had expected, perhaps a man who wore flowing robes or had a long beard and spoke in esoteric riddles. He had heard many stories from Suna about her teacher, the grandest of masters, who was able to move all of the energy of heaven into a single point with the power of his mind. The man in front of him seemed like the salt of the Earth, kind and gentle with native eyes that sparkled with a zest for life.

"I'm K'ete-t. Welcome to my home," he said once

everyone had taken their seat.

Suna introduced each person around the circle, both by their modern name and their name of origin.

Toby looked around the room in wonder, eyeing all of the portraits. One painting in particular caught his attention, a painting of an elderly Asian man with a long black beard, who wore cream-toned robes that hinted of nobility. The antiquity of the painting indicated that the man in the portrait lived long ago.

"Do you recognize him?" K'ete-t asked as he nodded his head toward the portrait.

"No." Toby shook his head.

"You seem to be the most curious about that particular portrait." K'ete-t shifted forward in his seat. "Can I ask why?"

"His face just seems to jump off the canvas at me like he's alive—in the portrait."

"Perhaps that is because his spirit is present with us, right now, in this room," Suna said, her eyes shining.

Toby looked around the room as if to perceive the spirit Suna spoke of.

"Would you like to hear about his life?" K'ete-t asked.

"Yes, very much," Toby answered.

K'ete-t spoke as if he were telling an ancient tale around a campfire. "Ten thousand years ago, in the region of East Asia, existed a spiritually matured, culturally advanced society, much like what we have heard about from the fables of Lemuria and Atlantis. This ancient society thrived for thousands of years under the rein of forty-seven consecutive ruling kings, known as the Dahngun ancestral line. The story begins with an enlightened king who traveled the lands of the Earth, searching for people to pass his knowledge on to. Fate brought him to the bear tribe in the region of Korea.

"In this tribe, there was one woman in particular who had a goodness inside her that desperately wanted to bloom. When the king entered the village, many people gathered, curious to meet a stranger from a far off land. The woman pushed through the crowd and the very instant that she saw his face, tears began to stream down her cheeks. She quickly wiped the tears away, startled by the experience of tears not linked to any particular emotion. What she didn't know was that those were the holy tears of her soul, for in him she perceived her own divinity reflected back to her. The voice of her soul resounded through every level of her being, calling for her to seek out the king and implore him to speak with her. *How can I become like him? Please show me the way.*

Her soul had beseeched the heavens for the

opportunity to grow, and the king, being connected with the essence of heaven, answered the call on heaven's behalf. He was so moved by the sincerity transmitted through her silent prayer that he accepted her as his student, and after twenty-one days of intensive training, she was enlightened to her divine essence as well. The king and the Bear-Lady eventually married and produced a son. That child was the first in the Dahngun line."

"The Bear-Lady?" Angeline suppressed a smirk. Her imagination conjured an image of a woman who was half bear, half human.

"She was called that because the bear was the totem animal of the tribe," K'ete-t explained. "Just as the eagle is the totem animal of your nation." He leaned back and smiled. "Perhaps your destiny will lead you to be known as the Eagle-Woman to future generations?"

Suna laughed, her eyes twinkling in delight. She touched Angeline's knee. "The story of the first Dahngun is assumed to be the founding myth of Korea. But it is more than a mere myth. It is history disguised as myth."

K'ete-t continued without missing a beat, "With the principles of the ChunBuKyung as its governing philosophy, this nation created a spiritual heritage for its people that ensured harmonious interactions. They were able to experience the magnificence of life because of their connection with heaven and Earth, as well as each other. Their cultural identity was rooted in the story of Mago and the celestial nature of human origin."

He pointed to the portrait of the Asian elder that Toby had been eyeing. "His name was Koyeulga. He was the son of the forty-seventh generation, as well as the final descendant of the Dahngun ancestral line. About two thousand years ago, before he finished his cycle of completion, or ascension, he closed his kingdom in order to protect the integrity of the sacred lineage. He was a very powerful man who became a very powerful being. He ascended with the sole purpose of initiating those ready to become enlightened. But as he left the physical realm, he closed the veil to the spiritual realm that had been opened by the first Dahngun, thereby separating the spiritual and material dimensions once more."

"Why he do that?" Leuters asked. It seemed a contradictory action for an enlightened master to take—especially one who had ascended so that he could help those remaining in the physical realm.

"It was a hard decision, but one he made because he felt a great responsibility to keep the integrity of the energies of heaven. There had been no separation between the physical and spiritual dimensions within his kingdom, but the culture of his society had become tainted by interaction with outside tribes—ones who didn't live according to the law of heaven. The corruption had begun in his village and the *Hong-Ik* spirit within his people had been tarnished."

Suna interjected, "*Hong-Ik* was the founding philosophy of that nation: *Widely benefiting all humanity, rightfully harmonize the world.*"

K'ete-t finished her thought. "While these words may not resonate in our current society, at the time they bore great meaning. If you think of it in terms of modern-day advertising, it's similar to the *Just do it* campaign synonymous with Nike. When you hear the phrase: *Just do it*, an entire philosophy and its precise meaning are conjured up in your mind. But if I came back nine thousand years from now, long after Nike had been forgotten, your question would be, *Just do* what?"

Everyone laughed. K'ete-t had an easy charm that only came with eons of experience. He continued, "The philosophy behind the Hong-Ik slogan is where the beauty lies, and why the community that held it as its founding principle was so special. Everyone knew themselves as an active and important part of the community. Each person strived to create mutually beneficial experiences with the people around them. No one person was on their own, nor did any one person benefit over another, regardless of skill or ability. It was a community in the truest sense of the word. Everyone contributed what they could because there was a natural compulsion in the heart to share." He clapped her hands together. "And that is what Hong-Ik means."

He leaned forward and spoke just above a whisper, "The time has come for the Hong-Ik spirit to be reignited in the hearts of humanity. The peak of the material civilization has come upon us and soon a new era will emerge. Spiritual values and material values will assimilate and all falsities and ignorance will evaporate like clouds in the sun when faced with the enlightened spirit of humanity. The lost spirit of Dahngun will bloom again and the veil will be lifted between the dimensions once more. That's why you've come back to the Earth. The Dahngun lineage is also your lineage and soon, all lineages will be revealed as one at their root."

"How do you know all of this?" Noah asked. He had been quietly considering everything that had been revealed.

"Even though most of the records have been destroyed, there are hints of this kingdom's existence in the culture. The Dahnguns have become mere characters in fairytales told to young children in bed-time stories. My knowledge of this great ancestral line comes, in large part, from experience. Though my tribe is Native American, when I follow my ancestral line all the way back, it leads to the Dahngun line—through you." He nodded his head toward Noah. "It was your line that this body descended from. All humanity leads back to your four lines." He indicated Noah, Toby, Leuters and Suna.

"There have been thousands of human origin stories handed down over the ages. Many have been forgotten. The ones that have prevailed have influenced the iden-tity of our species in ways that we can't even fathom. These stories are important because they explain where we come from, who we are at our root, how we relate to ourselves, each other, our planet, and our Creator."

Angeline tapped her chin as if thinking aloud. "A whole lot of people refer to the story of Eden in the Bible when conjuring an image of the first humans . . ."

K'ete-t answered, "And since that has been the prev-alent story for many generations, we've come to see our lives through a filter of dichotomy: good versus evil, brightness versus darkness, reward versus punish-ment, blessings versus curses. This story has influenced two thousand years of our history. As a species, we've been longing to resolve this story of us as fallen children competing to recover the love and blessings of a Father God whose face has turned away from anyone who doesn't offer penance. We turned God into a figure that prefers one race over another, pitting nations against each other with wars waged and blood spilled in the quest for salvation. The story modeled for us how we were to behave, telling us who we were, through story.

"You were never sent into exile as a form of punishment from an external power. You left Mago Castle of your own free will to protect it. It was choice. And, when another choice is made, we will be embraced by all life and return to the spirit of Mago Castle. We will remember who we really are. Divinity already exists within us; we just need to realize it. That is the revelation."

The tone of K'ete-t's voice changed. A holy authority echoed through the room, "You will free the people and end the oppression once and for all. Suna has brought you here to prepare for what you must face. I will give you every tool that I have so that you may see your opponent and know what you are fighting for. Once I have opened your sight, it cannot be undone. You will be forever changed. So, you must decide if this road is one that you are willing to take to the end."

"We have already decided. We are ready." Noah spoke for the group.

"Very well." K'ete-t nodded. "I will activate your sixth chakra, which will connect your perception to the realm beyond the five senses. The gifts that you have now will develop to their maximum capacity, and you will remember the history of the world from the mind of the cosmos." He picked up his drumstick.

Suna rose from her seat, discreetly turning the level of the light down. The room was aglow with the soft light from the crystal geode display cases. K'ete-t beat his drum, a slow and steady repetition that pounded through their every cell. He sang the ChunBuKyung in a cadence flavored by his years on the reservation and moved through many renditions of song and chant for a full twenty-four hours, without pause, without break. The ether crackled with particles of pure life as he led the five of them past the confines of illusion into the energy world of pure potentiality. Noah's assumption was correct: he was the master's master.

Leuters noticed that his perception dropped so completely inside of his body that each breath lasted for an eternity. With every exhale and inhale he died and was reborn, passing through his entire ancestral line to the conception of the Earth. He felt the essence of

Mago with a grandness that the confines of Angeline's human body couldn't express. She was huge. No matter how far his consciousness spread out, he could not find her end. She was the template for the billions of realities dreamed by the dreamers that she loved unconditionally.

While in the heightened state generated by the multiple streams of ChunBuKyung energy, Suna had a memory of the loss that Mago had experienced because of her love for her human children. When they broke their intuitive line to the law of the cosmos, they fell out of phase with the rest of the universe. The energy of heaven no longer circulated through humans in a free-flowing torus, because their energy line had been purposefully distorted to conceal their actions from the mind of the cosmos.

In order to allow her children time to exhaust their greed, she too had dropped out of phase with the heavens, and now sustained the planet with her own life force by tilting her axis, as her children had. Suna felt the sensation associated with this axis tilt; it was as if Mago were holding her breath underwater and was moments away from either drowning or bobbing back to the surface for another breath. Yet shifting her axis from twenty-four degrees back to zero, given the density on the planet, would be detrimental to humanity. Her children must let go of their heaviness and become light bodies again in order to shift back with her. And they had to do it fast. Time was running out. That was why Mago had come to deliver the principles of heaven, because she desperately wanted to prepare her children for the shift so that she might bring their souls with her when she phased.

Toby saw the dark fog that covered the Earth, like spilled ink. The planet was riddled with disembodied spirits attached to their stories of need and consumption. He saw that most humans on the planet were influenced by these dark spirits, who sought to control them in order to play out the karma they had created and who weighted down their souls.

Noah experienced what would happen to the souls who didn't become the light itself by the time the axis shifted. They would be cast off the planet and sucked into the black hole at the center of the galaxy, where their essence would unify and be compressed, only to blast out in a "big bang" that created a new universe of their own. They would exist, but not as sentient human beings.

Angeline saw her future and knew, without a doubt, the task that she was born to do. It was the ultimate purpose of her life. This fate both exhilarated and frightened her. But she saw that she had a choice, because even when things are destined, there is always a choice. Fulfilling her destiny would grow her soul to its completion, but deciding to fulfill this fate would cost her everything. Even after discovering that Mago was her oversoul, she never realized the part that she would play. It was bigger than she had imagined.

Time lost all meaning while K'ete-t drummed. They traveled through eons of memories across time and space, maturing thousands of years in mere days because they experienced every moment of time as if they had lived it themselves.

After two days of drumming, K'ete-t put his drumstick down. The silence roared. As he had promised, they knew what they were fighting and why it was so important that they win.

CHAPTER FIFTY-THREE

"There is a prophecy," K'ete-t said, his voice seasoned with the boom of cosmic authority. "Your place in this prophecy is to act as emissaries of the Mother of the Earth, her hands in the task of extinguishing the dark energies that cover the true spirit of humanity. She has waited for this moment for two thousand years," he said. "I will now reveal everything that I know.

"Three days from today, when the veils between the spiritual world and the material world are at their thinnest, there will be a great shift in the Astrological era that will make the Earth's magnetic field malleable. You must be on Bell Rock between the hours of four and six a.m.," he said. "You've practiced delivering the energy of heaven and the heart of the Earth in your lectures and trainings, but that was nothing compared to what you will now face. There are billions upon billions of souls who still require energetic healing, and dimensions of dark consciousness that you weren't even aware existed that still need to be resolved. Through you, Mother Mago will wipe the spiritual pains of her children away. However, during this process you will feel every layer, every pain, as if were your own, which will be a difficult burden to bear. You'll be tempted to step off of the path—putting the entire consciousness of the Earth in danger as well as your own human life," he warned. "The only way that you'll have the strength to succeed is if you unify together with one heart, one mind." He turned to Angeline and took her hand. They stood in front of the portrait of Mago that hung on the wall.

"You will be faced with a decision," he said.

"I have seen it, Seuseungnim," Angeline replied, casting her eyes to the ground. He squeezed her hand, tilted her chin up with his finger. She was unable to look away from the softness of the universe that she found in his eyes. It was the pillow of love that surrounds all life and holds it into form.

"Will you follow this path to the end?" he asked.

"Yes," she answered.

"Are you frightened?"

She smiled, not knowing how to respond. She could say *yes*, she could say *no*. Neither answer would change what she knew in her heart she must do. "I'm determined," she answered.

K'ete-t turned to the emissaries. "Before you stands a truly great soul. She is someone who has accepted responsibility for the fate of the planet. Let us offer the three bows: of love, honor, and gratitude."

When they offered the three traditional bows, Angeline's soul trembled. Witnessing her five closest friends offer the highest demonstration of sincerity made their souls shine like diamonds. In them, she saw her own soul. "You are also great souls on this mission with me," she said. She returned the three bows, very slowly, touching her forehead to the ground and allowing time to feel the importance of this moment. "Together we shall walk, until the very end."

"I'm with you," Suna said, embracing Angeline when she stood.

"As am I," Noah said, folding his arms around the two women.

"Me too," Leuters said, joining the group embrace.

Toby stepped forward and wrapped his arms around the group. His emotion was too deep to utter a word, but his soul declared its alliance with a thundering that ricocheted through all of eternity. K'ete-t joined the group and their minds unified as one. *The six gathered and there came a turning.* Angeline remembered the phrase from the ChunBuKyung. They had taken the final step. Each of their gifts, the heavenly items bequeathed to them, flashed with light and each of their seven chakras shone brilliantly as one.

"You will succeed," K'ete-t predicted. "You are the hope for humanity."

***

The hot air balloon carried them through the sky. Noah had never traveled by hot air balloon. K'ete-t had offered it to them so that they could return to Sedona without detection by the highway patrol or governmental authorities who surely were looking to identify them at the airports. It was important that they make it to Bell Rock at the precise time specified. There wasn't room for any delay; the Earth would shift, whether they were ready or not. Noah watched the landscape transform from valley to mountains. This planet was breathtaking. As the sun began to set, they touched down in Sedona. The protective energy of its native lands seemed to wrap around them, promising to guard them until their last moment.

"We'll be walking to Bell Rock from here," Suna said, after they had landed.

For the past three days, they had engaged in a bowing meditation. The one thousand bows per day had left their minds clear and their hearts filled with hope, as Angeline was reminded every time she took a step, their legs stiff.

"I need to make a phone call," Noah said when they passed the convenience store on Highway 179. They had discarded their cell phones so that they wouldn't be tracked. He put the coins in the phone and dialed.

"Hello?" Annie, his daughter answered the call.

"Sweetheart?" Noah's heart leapt in his chest.

"Papa? Where are you? People have been looking for you," she said, her voice laden with concern. "Are you okay?"

"I'm good, Annie," he assured her. "I need you to do something."

"Anything," she said.

"I need you and Bill to listen to the CD that I gave you tomorrow morning from precisely seven a.m. until nine a.m." He had sent her a CD of the ChunBuKyung last year at Christmas. He wasn't sure that his idea would work, but he needed to do something to ensure that his daughter and son-in-law's spirits weren't tossed from the Earth when the axis shifted straight. In his vision, he had seen the fate of the spirits that didn't ascend with the Earth. Their karma would nullify, and they would have to start life from scratch. From "big bang" to amoeba and, if they were lucky, after millions of years a sentient being again.

"Daddy?" she asked.

"It's important," he said urgently. "Do you still have it?"

"Yes." Her voice was strange, distant. Noah knew that she was trying to puzzle out this most perplexing request. Her father was on the run with known fugitives, and he had called her to ask that she and her husband listen to a track from a CD that he had given her. It didn't make sense.

"I can't explain the purpose in a way that you'll understand, but it is important. Promise me."

"I promise," she said. "Are you coming home?"

"Soon, darling. I will be home soon. I love you." And he did. She was his little girl. She always would be.

He hung up the phone and he, Angeline, Suna, Toby, and Leuters resumed their journey to Bell Rock.

"Any regrets?" Toby asked the group.

"I wish that K'ete-t could be here," Suna said. She knew that it was important that he stay with the next generation of masters, but the part of her that would always hold him as her mentor wished he could be with her in this most daunting task.

"Wish I tried harder to give MFS to world," Leuters said.

"I wish that I'd had some ice cream," Angeline confessed.

Everyone laughed. Noah laughed with the others, but his mind was fixed on only one thing. Leading them safely to the top of Bell Rock. It was almost time.

CHAPTER FIFTY-FOUR

The night was eerily quiet. The common sounds of the dark desert night were absent: the crickets were silent, the seasonal rattle of the cicadas was still, there were no coyote howls in the distance, even the wind seemed to be holding its breath. The only sound that could be heard was their footsteps on the rock, which seemed to echo through the still night.

"Strange," Leuters said.

Suna nodded in agreement. It even felt like the life had been sucked out of the air. She had trouble catching a full breath, which she assumed was because she was nervous. But perhaps it was more.

"Something doesn't feel right." Toby looked around them, on high alert.

"Let's just get to the top as soon as we can,"

Noah advised them hurriedly.

This hike was much more difficult than it had been in the past. There was an unseen repellent force pushing down on them. They felt as if they walked uphill against a hundred pounds of added gravity. A twig snapped under Toby's foot. Everyone jumped reflexively.

"Just a stick," he laughed.

Suna exhaled, trying to calm her heartbeat. She didn't want to give into paranoia, but she felt as if someone was watching them.

"Does anyone else feel like the boogey man is going to jump out at us?" Toby joked.

"Yes," Suna answered. She could still hear her own heartbeat thunder in her ears.

Angeline feared that what they would face would make the boogey man seem as harmless as the Easter bunny. Her stomach churned. "What time is it?"

Noah looked at his watch. "Four o'clock."

Angeline peered into the dark sky. It felt like the infinite ceiling had dropped and the once distant space had closed in upon them. It was utterly claustrophobic.

They reached the top of the mountain and sat in a circle formation, with Angeline in the center. "What should we do?" she asked.

"We wait," Suna answered.

***

There's an ever-present rumble that surrounds all life. It's a sound so constant that the brain has deemed it nonessential to survival and therefore has edited it from conscious perception. But the moment that this soundless sound came to a halt, every single person on the planet noticed its stillness. It was dead silent.

The perpetual propulsion of the planet rotating around its axis came to a standstill and the Earth quaked to a sudden stop. Angeline looked around the still dark morning and a chill ran up her spine.

"Now," Suna exclaimed urgently, and the silence atop Bell Rock was filled with the chant of the Chun Bu Kyung.

K'ete-t had been very clear about the process that they would follow. They would chant the ChunBuKyung ceaselessly for two hours, keeping the ether above Bell Rock clear while the core of the Earth shifted to its zero point within the center of the planet, in preparation for the most dramatic axis shift in history. From twenty-four degrees to zero, all at once.

Angeline's eyes began to phase, enabling her to witness another dimension. It was a holographic dimension where physical form lost density. She watched her friends, who chanted the ChunBuKyung, and understood the purpose of speaking its eighty-one characters. When the code was chanted, it created a vibrational resonance that called the energy of the ChunBuKyung into them, through the tops of their heads. Speaking the words was almost like dialing the direct phone number to the creator of the cosmos. When the code was recognized, the line was created, and instant communication with the cosmos was possible.

As each person in the circle filled with the light of God, it circulated through their auras in an ever-moving torus that spun and flashed like cosmic fireworks. The five overlapping tori formed the sacred geometric shape—the seed of life.

"It's working." Angeline saw that each person had lost shape and form. Only light bodies existed, filled with the blinding energy of God. Though their shapes had become invisible, their heavenly items, the gifts bequeathed to their souls, shone brightly. Leuters had become a sword of light; Suna, a golden bell. Toby became a mirror that reflected the truth, and since the people he was reflecting had become God, the mirror amplified the existing light. Noah's chakra pendant glimmered all of the colors of the rainbow.

Angeline knew that when she looked at her own soul, she would see the aquamarine crystal. What she didn't expect was to find that her body hovered above the ground. With each recitation of the ChunBuKyung, she was lifted higher through the center of the torus. When she reached the top of this crystalline globe of ChunBuKyung energy, she looked upon the land with the eyes of spirit. And it was beautiful.

This is our kingdom. This Earth is the kingdom of the children of Mago, the children of heaven. Every detail had been imbued with love because it was created by the mind of God.

Like a lover's palm, her awareness spread to caress valleys and mountains, oceans and forests. Her consciousness grew to encompass the entire planet. The sound of the ChunBuKyung filled her ears, the celestial soundtrack for her ever-expanding mind.

And then she felt it. A snag in the fluidity. A tear in the collective field of reality. The entrance to a sub-reality, the underbelly of existence. She didn't know what was on the other side of this tear in reality, but she could sense that whatever it was, it wasn't good. This was it. The reason that she had been born. This moment was the reason that K'ete-t had offered her the three bows and called her a great soul. But she had to choose. She heard Mago's voice echo in her heart,

Invite it to return to you. You have to be brave. I am

with you. You are not alone. Call every bit of it into you, and I will help you. But you must claim it now, in this moment.

Angeline followed Mago's instructions with her heart. With one thought, her wish was granted. She touched the heart of the darkness and called it to her.

Don't be afraid of any creation. Whatever has been created, you have the power to uncreate. You have the authority, as a human being made from the breath of God. Anything else that you think is a lie. You have to trust yourself to fix it.

Angeline looked at the darkness that was closing in on them. It whirred like billions of angry bats thirsting for blood. And she knew that the dark mass was composed of every moment of suffering that had been created since the separation. She wasn't sure what she was going to do with the darkness when it reached them. She only knew that she had to face it. She took a deep breath and waited, bracing herself for what was to come.

CHAPTER FIFTY-FIVE

A billowing cloud of black closed in upon them, from all directions. Angeline had called every bit of unconscious energy on the planet to them. And it had come. Thousands of wandering souls, ancestors bound to descendants, spirits chained to the land by traumatic death, lost between realms, every thought, emotion, curse, or miscreation that had occurred since the beginning of time and had not been forgiven or resolved rushed toward them at breakneck speed. Within seconds, the darkness hit Angeline, smacking into her and knocking her to the ground, falling through the center column of the torus, crashing into the rock. The crystalline aura around the group buckled under the blow and shattered like glass, leaving everyone vulnerable to attack.

"No!" Noah hollered.

The spirits dove to feast on them, consuming the light of their goodness like ravenous wolves. The smell of them was putrid; it burned the nose.

Leuters swatted his body, attempting to deflect the sting of the spirits as they tried to attach to him. They buzzed like hornets. Millions of entities clamored, each demanding the volume of light needed to restore their fragmentation. Toby gagged when a spirit attached itself to his face and sucked the soul energy through his nose and eyes. He retched as the karma was devoured from his soul.

"How we can fight them?" Leuters hollered.

"More energy. Chant the ChunBuKyung now!" Suna yelled.

"It's too much," Toby protested. Another spirit that looked like a jellyfish attached itself to his liver. He winced and held his side.

Angeline had never experienced this grueling level of spiritual torment. Yet because of the heightened level of pain, she suddenly realized something pivotal. Once she accepted the pain, it didn't hurt. It was her resistance to the pain that generated the feeling of pain. She stood, wrapped in spirits, screaming to her friends. "It's not real!" Nobody understood. "It's not real!" Angeline yelled, again. Her friends twisted on the ground in torment.

She couldn't understand why she was the only one who understood. It was so clear. She looked at the faces of her friends who had come with her to save the world, and her heart overflowed with love. She didn't speak a word. She just let the love pour from her heart.

Something shifted. The love that her heart generated softened the darkness. The spirits didn't have to clamor to consume the light, they were hit with a wave of it. Angeline realized that just chanting the ChunBuKyung wasn't enough. A recitation of even the most powerful of texts chanted with fear wasn't going to save the world. It was love. It was her love.

"Angeline," Toby said in warning. He had read her thoughts.

"This isn't a battle that can be won by fist, nor by mind. Only love will save us," she said. Love was her power. She had thought it was healing. She had been wrong.

"No." Leuters reached through the milling spirits to grab her arm.

"You've done enough. You brought me here, you protected me," she said, softly.

Suna and Noah understood her intention only from her admission. "Angeline," Noah protested.

"Without even knowing it, I've been waiting for this moment my entire life." She touched Noah's face. "Teach them to dream a better dream." She turned and ran to the farthest edge of the cliff.

"No." Toby chased after her. She ignored him.

"In me, you will find your resolution." Her voice rose loudly, calling the spirits. Yet it wasn't the sound of her voice that caught their attention, it was the vibration of pure love that poured from her heart. This vibration was the cure to every illness, the light to every dark, the answer to every question. It was the fulfillment of every lack in this world, the only thing that was truly important. *Love.*

Within seconds, she was covered with a dark mass composed of every spirit who had ever existed who was sick with anger, disappointment, attachment, and devastation since the beginning of time.

Toby tried to pull her free, but the sting of the spirits still stung him because he hadn't overcome the illusion, as Angeline had. The sound of their consumption echoed through the space like thunder. Soon, there would be nothing left of her.

And she gave of herself willingly. Because she finally knew love.

CHAPTER FIFTY-SIX

Bill stuffed his feet into his slippers and shuffled to the living room where his fiancée, Annie, was fiddling with the stereo.

"Doesn't your dad know that Saturday is my only day to sleep in?" he grumbled.

"Just lie on the couch." Annie hit the Play button and the sound of chanting poured from speakers.

"It's just weird," he protested.

"I promised him," she said.

"Can't we just pretend that we did it?"

"You didn't hear his voice," Annie said. Her father was a serious man. He was intentional with everything that he said and did. She only knew one thing in this world—if her father asked her to do something, there was a good reason.

She settled on the couch next to Bill and cozied into his side.

"Are we supposed to do something?"

"Just listen, I guess."

He kissed her cheek and pulled her close. Before long he was dozing.

Annie wrapped herself in his arms and listened to the harmonic voices chant, accompanied by the soft purr of Bill's snores, and soon she too fell asleep. She was awakened by the sensation of a pop at the top of her head. Her vision flashed white, even though her eyes were closed. She felt like she was going to faint, even though she was already lying down. Her blood ached as it passed through her veins and her muscles contracted, as if she was suffering from an instantaneous bout of the flu.

Bill shifted beneath her. A huff of discomfort escaped his lips. He moaned a little and turned over, shifting her to the edge of the couch. She turned to spoon him, wrapping her arms tightly around him.

A blood-curdling scream sounded through their open window and reverberated through the living room. All traces of her illness were forgotten. She jumped to her feet. Bill was not far behind her.

"What was that?" he asked, eyes wild.

Another scream.

"Mr. Bickles," Annie breathed, her heart pounding in her ears.

It took them approximately six seconds to reach the neighbor's front door. The hollow sound of Bill's fist pounding on the door sounded throughout the neighborhood.

"Mr. Bickles?" he yelled, urgently.

Mr. Bickles was a mean old man. Selfish and greedy. Curt and rude. He was the type of neighbor who measured the length of your grass and reported it to the home owners' association if it was a millimeter beyond the suggested height. He was nosy too. Bill often caught him suspiciously peeking out the window every time headlights crossed his blinds. He looked in Annie and Bill's garbage bins on trash day, keeping tabs on his African American neighbors, sifting through discarded toothpaste tubes and empty cans of crushed tomatoes. He even called the police once when a holiday party that they hosted ran later than his liking. Bill often found himself counting to ten when he would hear Mr. Bickles snap at his wife for something trivial, like leaving the door open while she carried numerous loads of groceries into the house while he sat in his Lazy Boy recliner, watching the game, or perhaps taking too long to bring him his drink.

Mrs. Bickles was a cute little old lady. She was rotund with rosy cheeks. She flitted. Most of her time was spent scurrying about, trying not to evoke the wrath of her mean old husband. She seemed to love him though. Bill was befuddled that such a sweet lady ended up with a complete scrooge. Opposites attracted, he supposed.

When Bill kicked down the door, he froze.

If he hadn't seen it with his own eyes, he never would have believed it.

Mr. Bickles was twisted on the ground, screaming as if he was dying.

Death may have been a better fate.

His face was purple, eyes wide, mouth open in a gaping scream. He pulled at his skin as he writhed in torment. Impossibly, Bill could see Mr. Bickles's nervous system through his skin, as if he had developed X-ray vision. Black tar oozed through its many branches and flowed up his face, coagulating in a network that tangled like yarn over the crown of his head. A light shone from his brainstem through the darkness, casting shadows across his face.

If that weren't disturbing enough, the look of sheer terror in Mr. Bickles's wide eyes was something that Bill would never forget, even if he lived a thousand years.

And the smell. The acrid scent of greed and desperation. The musty scent of an enclosed chamber with no circulation, no sunshine, the smell of a dying soul.

Annie rushed to help Mr. Bickles but the smell made her gag uncontrollably.

"It burns!" Mr. Bickles screeched, pounding his head with his fists.

The light slowly moved through Mr. Bickles's head.

He screamed again as the light pushed upward, bursting through the dark conglomeration of cords. A halo as bright as the sun birthed itself from the top of his head, hovering two inches above. It shone down upon Mr. Bickles like a spotlight from heaven.

"It burns!" Mr. Bickles swatted at his flesh as if trying to put out a fire across the entire length of his body. Swirls of darkness, like evil tadpoles swimming, like leeches from the underworld, moved about his flesh, scurrying under the light before they were burned to ashes under the brilliance of the halo.

Bill held his breath and knelt beside him, but didn't know how to help. He'd never seen anything like it.

"Call 911!" he yelled.

Annie ran to the kitchen and dialed the phone. She covered her nose and watched from the doorway. Bill stepped away from Mr. Bickles to catch his breath, placing the neckline of his sweater over his nose. He was determined to withstand the choking odor and offer some help.

With a final scream, Mr. Bickles's body slumped. Mr. Bickles had passed out.

His lifetime of darkness exhausted, his skin glowed with health. His face looked surprisingly plump and youthful. The deep breath of an infant moved his belly rhythmically. For the first time since Bill met Mr. Bickles, he looked peaceful. Like a sleeping angel having the sweetest dream in the history of histories.

CHAPTER FIFTY-SEVEN

Only when the dark spirits that suffocated the group lifted was Leuters able to identify the putrid brimstone scent they carried as the same that permeated the Mexican federal prison where he had been incarcerated. As soon as he identified the familiar smell, his mind clicked into the realm of the cosmic mind, and though his body remained on Bell Rock, his awareness was instantly transported to the prison.

He saw all of the cells in the prison simultaneously. Some of the inmates he recognized from his time in the correctional institution, but many he had never seen before. He watched from the perspective of the all-knowing, all-seeing cosmic mind as both prisoners and guards alike shook in seizure. Their bodies flounced violently, both orange jumpsuits and tan uniforms, as dark energy birthed itself through every orifice in their bodies. It looked like a scene from Revelations, where people twisted in torment while burning eternally in a lake of fire. Not every person in the prison suffered from this demonic birthing process, however. A few of the prisoners slept soundly on their bunks, wrapped in threadbare wool blankets that were dirty from years of use.

Leuters's mind traveled around the globe, and he watched varying expressions of the same scene. Somewhere on the other side of the world, speaking in a language that Leuters didn't recognize, a self-proclaimed prophet dressed in holy garb vomited black spiritual tar while standing at the front of an auditorium.

He watched as every person on the planet expelled the dark delusions that haunted their bodies and minds, realizing that most people, even the relatively normal, were in fact very spiritually ill. The darkness rose like smoke, hanging in the ether. The poor, the rich, the famous, leaders of churches, government officials—there were no exceptions. Except one: a small town in New Zealand where kids played hide-and-seek. He watched as each child let out a small cough and released a puff of gray smoke, then resumed their game, unaware of the commotion rocking the rest of the world.

It lasted for only three minutes. And then the world was silent again. People looked about them in a daze, not understanding what had just happened. They rubbed their eyes as if waking from a bad dream.

His perception clicked back into Sedona, where all of the darkness, from around the globe, had traveled. He watched the spirits whir, loud and violent, wrapping around and passing through the brother he had known in this lifetime. His brother fell to his knees and screamed. Every horror that had been created on the Earth passed through his consciousness in a stream of images. The darkness demanded to be both known and experienced until it had found its resolution. But, in him, it wouldn't find the light that it sought. His brother screamed curses and banged his head against the ground—as if trying to knock himself out.

"Jiso!" Angeline cried. The alarm in her voice indicated that she had witnessed the same scene. She turned her head quickly and locked eyes with Leuters, though he could hardly see her through the cloud of darkness that shrouded her. "Come to me! Every single one of you—come to me!" she commanded the proximal darkness. Her voice boomed with such authority that Leuters's body shook in response. Within seconds, the remaining darkness in the small mountain town rushed forth and engulfed her. Jiso had been freed. He dropped his head into his hands and wept, thanking a God that he neither saw nor felt.

Leuters breathed a sigh of relief. He saw his brother for what he was. His soul had never matured. He was like a child, burdened by the consequences of untold lifetimes of bad choices.

In a startling contrast, Angeline had offered to shoulder the burden that Jiso had created, but was incapable to carry on his own. Tears streamed down Leuters's cheeks. Simply witnessing the maturity that she displayed made his soul reach to do the same. She had taken responsibility for the darkness, whether it was hers or not, and he was determined to do the same. He turned to find her, but she had completely disappeared from sight. She stood at the center of a hurricane of terror and darkness.

Leuters remembered the vow that he had made to her: *I will protect you.* He looked around wildly, trying to formulate a plan. He called to the darkness, just as Angeline had, "Come to me!"

The darkness did not move. It shifted around her, clamoring like moths to the flame.

"Come to me!" he yelled again, this time more

emphatically. He jumped up and down and waved his arms. "Come to me . . . come to me . . ." he cried desperately when he saw that his plea had been unnoticed.

"We have to help her!" Toby hollered over the deafening sound. "We can't leave her alone; there will be nothing left of her."

"I'll go," Noah yelled. He braced himself to run straight into the darkness.

"I'm going with you," Suna called after him.

Noah stopped, turned around and shook his head. "No," was all he said.

"I have to," she said. "For myself, for my humanity, for my world."

Ignoring Noah's protest, Leuters wrapped his arm around her, an attempt to shield her, as they ran into the darkness without a moment of hesitation. Toby and Noah were fast on their heels. They didn't know what they would face; they only knew that they needed to help Angeline—for themselves, for their humanity, for their world.

CHAPTER FIFTY-EIGHT

When they stepped into the darkness, they stepped into another world. It wasn't the angry hell that they had anticipated seeing when they broke past the boundary of black spirits that clamored against each other with the frenzy of sperm trying to break the surface of an egg. Beneath the undulating mass of spirits was an iridescent capsule that looked like a big and beautiful soap bubble.

Angeline stood at its center. She was no longer recognizable as the woman that they had known. She was a goddess whose translucent form was a soft golden light the color of sunshine sparkling on honey. Birds of every shape and color in the rainbow flew around her, flitting in and out of existence. Each time one of the dark spirits would push its way past the gelatinous field that surrounded her, it would fly into her chest and she would laugh, as if she were being tickled. Moments later, the spirit would reemerge as a magnificent soul bird that whirled around her, flapping joyously before disappearing from this realm to another.

When she saw her friends, her smile grew twice its size and the golden energy emanating from her heart surged, wrapping around them like warm and cozy blankets.

Leuters, who had braced himself to face every horror in hell, cried out in relief. He fell to his knees and bowed his head. The others followed. Before them stood the holiest of souls, whose love had transformed all the hells on Earth into her own personal heaven. It was no wonder all of the dark and discarded spirits clamored to be near her: in her eyes, they weren't evil things to be rebuked. They were precious, accepted, and loved. And because they were shown love, they remembered love and recovered their original spirit.

Toby's body shook. Standing in the presence of her light raised him through many levels of purification. He had thought that he had been purified to his absolute zero point, but saw that he hadn't. There were a few foundational layers of his ego that he had hidden from the light because he was ashamed for them to be seen under it. But now that this blinding light shone upon him, he was free from the prison he had created to conceal those few actions from being known. And the simple action of allowing himself to be seen was the repentance required to restore his soul to its original splendor.

"The light never intended to punish you," Angeline said, answering his thought. "You created your own punishment—which was to block the light—because you felt guilty. The light never needed your penance, nor does it need you to pay for your mistakes. It only requires that you be willing to see them. In the precise moment of witnessing, you are forgiven."

Toby had only just met another being on the Earth who embodied this same level of unconditional and transformative love. "Seuseungnim," he breathed. He had heard Suna refer to K'ete-t by the same title, but hadn't fully understood the word. It wasn't simply a title—it was the recognition of a profoundly intimate connection. Though there have been many great teachers who had existed throughout time, he recognized this woman as *his* Seuseungnim. In this moment, on this day, in all of eternity . . . he fell in love. Not in the way that a man falls in love with a woman, but in the way that all of heaven loves the Earth. His soul yielded, and he basked in the greatness of the pure existence this woman embodied.

"The curtain has been drawn on the material world and a new era has begun. But you haven't finished yet," she said.

"Finished what?" Noah asked.

"The restoration of the Earth."

"But, isn't that what you have done?"

"I have absolved the darkness. Now you must return and lead the world into the era of—"

"You won't come back with us?" Toby despaired.

She looked upon him with holy compassion, understanding why he despaired. "I will be with you, but this world is no longer mine."

CHAPTER FIFTY-NINE

All was silent except for the echo of a celestial song-bird tweeting from another realm. The particles in Angeline's field looked like tiny iridescent soap bubbles that reflected the light of a golden Buddha upon their surface. It was this golden Buddha that Angeline had seen in her vision at Cathedral Rock. It was the aura that surrounded the Earth, the essence of Mago, and it was the place where she belonged. The image of the golden Buddha was the thought mirrored in every particle within her sphere of influence—the entire surface of the globe.

An enormous vibration shook the ground and the Earth shuddered as its axis shifted back to its zero point. With every degree traveled, Angeline's energy field got bigger and brighter until her blinding light turned to fire. Noah, Suna, Leuters and Toby stood at the center of these celestial flames of heaven, and Noah recalled the old biblical story of the burning bush. It was a fire that did not burn. Because they had been purified, the power of the flames flickered in glorious waves of ecstasy. They stood at the center of the sun and, for a moment, became the sun itself.

The shudder of the Earth's axis shift stopped. The thundering soundless sound of the Earth's rotation began again—a sound as comforting as a mother's song to a baby. The holy flames that had engulfed them ascended into the sky, like a great golden phoenix of light that carried Angeline's spirit on its wings.

For the second time today, Angeline's four partners-in-consciousness fell to their knees with reverent hearts. They watched as her soul, transformed into a golden phoenix of light, flew around Bell Rock three times, trailing golden particles behind her that twinkled like confetti.

They witnessed the process of her completion, as if watching the mind-screen of the cosmos. It was her spiritual birth—the transition from individual to one, from human to God, from something to nothing, yet everything at the same time. The sky opened as if a zipper had been pulled and the soul of Mago, the golden

Buddha, all of the heavens, and every being who had made the same journey welcomed the spirit of this great human being, whose love for mankind was ultimate.

As her spirit evolved, her consciousness spread around the Earth, like honey. Time and space ceased to exist for an eternal moment. Her friends gazed into the sky where she had once been, and though they could no longer see her, they felt her essence wrap around all of humanity. The field surrounding the planet shone brighter with her added light. She had made it home, as all will, in their own time. She existed above thought and emotion in the place where the pure and eternal beingness of God stretches infinitely in all directions.

Tears of gratitude poured down Toby's cheeks as he looked into the sky. Suna dropped her face into her trembling hands and cried tears of the ultimate love in her heart. Noah looked around with wonderment at the new Earth whose every particle gleamed in Technicolor. And Leuters touched his forehead to the ground and thanked the spirit of the Earth, Mother Mago, for all that she had done.

The voice of Mother Mago echoed through the sky.

"Chun-Hwa is the path to become one with the immortal soul of God. I exist here, and always, as death does not exist. The world is ready for the veils to be lifted. Black clouds no longer cover the sky. A new *sun* will shine upon the Earth. A shattered light returns in five vessels. This is the Tao of enlightenment, the *Hong-Ik Human*, and the message of BOS.

"Prepare for the return of Mago Castle."

EPILOGUE:

THE STORY OF

MAGO CASTLE

There is an ancient creation story passed down from the part of the Earth that is now Korea and recorded in the *Budoji*, an ancient text recorded by Jaesang Park, a scholar of the Shila dynasty. Though this story originates from the ancient history of Korea, it doesn't speak to the history of Korea but rather to the history of humanity.

According to the *Budoji*, in the beginning, before heaven, nothing existed except for the flowing rhythm of the cosmos. The text cites that Mago, the Mother of the Earth, was created through the undulations of the cosmic rhythm, called Yulyo. Additionally, all of the stars in the sky were also created through countless reincarnations of this friction. Yulyo was called forth again and again, first creating water, then land that existed in the midst of the water. Energy, Fire, Water and Earth came into being, combining in varied increments to form night and day, the four seasons and all of the richness of the Earth. A paradise was also created, located on the most precious lands, known as Mago Castle.

Mother Mago then coupled with the energy of heaven, creating two celestial daughters, Gunghee and Sohee, to help with the task of creating all living things on the Earth. Just as Mother Mago had, both daughters created children of their own. Four human daughters maintained the yin, or female, tones and vibrations of heaven, while four human sons maintained the yang, or male, tones. The names of the women are long forgotten, but the names of the men are remembered as: *Hwanggung* (Yellow Child), who was charged with caring for Earth; *Baekso* (White Child), who maintained the balance of Energy; Chunggung (Blue Child), who maintained the Water; and *Heukso* (Black Child), charged with the task of managing Fire.

The descendants of these men and women formed

four tribes in Mago Castle, where all lived in harmony with one another and the Earth. These original humans sustained their life force by drinking from the milk of the Earth, which sprung from the ground in Mago Castle, and they were quite different from the humans of today. Because they survived only on the milk given freely by Mago, all humans had a pure heart as well as clear blood and energy, which ensured that their *ki* energy flowed freely within the body, also allowing them to hear and understand heaven.

With their connection to both heaven and the Earth, they also had the power to create matter from energy easily. The people of Mago Castle were able to turn their bodies into pure, golden energy in order to preserve them after finishing their daily work, and therefore could communicate without sound, travel without form, and live eternally.

This idyllic existence found in Mago Castle did not last. As the people multiplied, the milk of the Earth could not sustain the ever-expanding population.

One day, a man named Jiso from Baekso's (White Child's) tribe, went to a well to drink, but the well was too small to nourish the number of people who had gathered. He yielded to others five times, when at last he passed out from hunger. When he awoke, lightheaded, he ate a grape from a nearby vine, receiving enough energy from it to survive. The grape contained all five flavors: sweet, sour, salty, bitter, and spicy/savory.

When Jiso told others that the grape was good, many people from the four tribes tried the grapes out of curiosity. The eating of fruits and grains began, but this was soon prohibited since this food was not pure like the milk provided directly by Mago. By ingesting nourishment other than Mago's milk, people's connection to their Mother weakened.

The necessity of creating an external rule also weakened the connection between the people of Mago Castle and heaven. In having to follow a rule, they broke the rule of *"not having rules and just following the intuitive sound of heaven."* They became further distracted from the sound of heaven as they became more and more absorbed in the sensual pleasure of taste and the other four basic human senses.

The individuals who chose to no longer be sustained by Mago's milk became deaf to the subtle sounds of heaven and their resonance no longer matched the pure energy of Mago Castle. This corruption created a disharmony that eventually required that they relocate outside of the paradise. Some who left missed the way that they had formerly lived in Mago Castle, especially the nourishment from Mago's milk. To re-capture a taste of the milk, they dug the land near the borders of Mago Castle, destroying the sources that supplied the wells within the paradise. When the wells started to dry, the remaining members of Mago Castle began to eat fruits and plants for fear of hunger, and they also lost their purity.

As the eldest son of Mago, Hwanggung felt a huge responsibility for this tragedy and repented to Mago. He made the decision to leave Mago Castle with the remaining members of the community in order to prevent the complete destruction of their precious paradise. He made an oath to one day help human be-ings return to their state of being, so that they might recover their seamless connection with heaven and the Earth. In preparation for that day, he created sacred markers of heaven's law so that the principles com-monly known in the time of Mago Castle could be re-membered when the era for restoration had come. He gave a copy of the sacred markers to each of the tribe leaders and taught all of the people how to survive in the world outside of Mago Castle, such as how to make food from kudzu root.

Finally, he ordered all the tribes to go their sepa-rate ways, and they spread to each corner of the Earth.

Chunggung went to the areas that are known today as China, Japan, and Central and South America; Baekso went to the Middle East and Europe; Heukso went to parts of what are now Indonesia, India, and Africa; and Hwanggung took the most dangerous route through Siberia, East Asia, and North America. This choice showed his determination to keep his oath by choosing and enduring hardship.

Since that time, the people of the world have gone through periods of both darkness and enlightenment as they struggle to recover the laws of heaven and live from the heart of their true selves. The ways of Mago Castle have been passed down through spiritual traditions, such as Sundo in Korea, as both spiritual principles and energy practices that allow the return to the divine state of energy resonance that human beings embodied when first sounded into being at Mago Castle. While this story may have been long forgotten, the state of Mago Castle exists in each of our hearts, waiting to be remembered.

ACKNOWLEDGMENTS

I've stood on the shoulders of giants. I thank every single person who encouraged me as I wrote this book, especially my mentor, the teacher who single-handedly helped me breathe the life back into my soul, Ilchi Lee.

Not only did meeting you change my life, but without you, this book would have never been possible. It was you who shared the incredible story of Mago Castle with me, it was you who helped me believe (like, really believe) that a better world was possible. You inspired me to write this story and pushed me to overcome my limitations and become a better storyteller. Even though I'm a writer, I'll never be able to express with words my gratitude. I thank you for working tirelessly for the last thirty years to popularize enlightenment— bringing it down from the mountaintops and into the masses in so simple a form as your Brain Education methods, so that one day this experience would be available to a young woman like me.

I am also grateful for encountering the story of Mago Castle. Having grown up in Western culture, with the story of Eden and the fall of man as my moral compass, I was deeply captivated by the possibility of Mago Castle, an origin where enlightenment was as natural a progression as going through puberty, or growing a mustache. This ideal community, where everyone grew into their divinity and lived harmoniously within the fluid energies of heaven, Earth, and all living beings, inspires me still.

The process of stepping into the hearts and minds of the various characters in this book, and really living through the process of humanity recovering its original, beautiful character, gave me hope and helped me realize how truly close we are to changing the experience of life on this Earth.

So much love went into this novel. I'd also like to thank my dream team: Tracy Seybold and Mark Rhynsburger for combing through the manuscript and crossing all of my i's and dotting all of my t's; Seula Song and Michelle Seo for the many, many hours of encouragement and translation; Michela Mangiaracina for her impeccable editorial support; Oliver Nasteski and Vanessa Maynard for a cover that I could stare at for hours and hours and never tire; and Eunjung Shin, Jiyoung Oh, and Eunjin Lim for their guidance on the spiritual heritage of Korea.

I'd also like to officially take this opportunity to thank every hurdle that has made me cower in the face of its difficulty, for it was you that helped me discover the great strength within me.

And most of all, I'd like to thank the Earth for feeding me, giving me a place to live, and for hosting this spectacular story of humanity. I've learned a lot since I've been here, and I promise to roll up my sleeves and do all that I can to restore your original splendor. You are magnificent.